Dracula

DRACULA

Bram Stoker

Abridged by Doris Dickens

CLASSICS

This edition first published
in Armada in 1988
This edition published 1993 by
Diamond Books
77-85 Fulham Palace Road
Hammersmith, London, W6 8JB

Printed and bound in Great Britain

Chapter I

JONATHAN HARKER'S JOURNAL

3 May. Bistritz, Transylvania. Left Munich at 8.35 p.m., on 1st May arriving at Vienna early next morning; should have arrived at 6.46, but train was an hour late. Budapest seems a wonderful place, from the glimpse which I got of it from the train and the little I could walk through the town. I was afraid to go very far from the station as we had arrived late and would start again as near the correct time as possible. I felt that we were leaving the West and entering the East. The most western of splendid bridges over the Danube, which is here of noble width and depth, reminded us of the time when this country was under Turkish rule.

We left in pretty good time, and came after nightfall to Klausenburgh. Here I stopped for the night at the Hotel Royale. I had for supper a chicken done up some way with red pepper, which was very good but thirsty. The waiter told me it was a national dish. We spoke in

German and I was thankful that I knew a little as I don't know how I should be able to get on without it.

My mission is to visit a nobleman, Count Dracula, who lives in a castle in the east of the country, high up in the Carpathian mountains. I have searched such maps as I could find for the exact locality of Castle Dracula, but find only Bistritz, which Count Dracula has informed me is his nearest town. Apparently it is quite a well-known place.

I did not sleep well in Klausenburgh for I had all sorts of queer dreams, and there was a dog howling all night under my window. The train started a little before eight, and all day we seemed to dawdle through a country which was full of beauty of every kind. At every station there were groups of people wearing various kinds of national dress, for there are many different races in this part of eastern Europe.

It was on the dark side of twilight when we got to Bistritz, which is a very interesting old place. Being practically on the frontier – for the Borgo Pass leads from it into Bukovina – it has had a very stormy existence, and it certainly shows marks of it. There have been great fires, war, famine and disease.

Count Dracula had directed me to go to the Golden Krone Hotel, which I found, to my great delight, to be thoroughly old-fashioned, for of course I wanted to see all I could of the ways of the country. I was evidently expected, for when I got near the door I faced a cheery-looking elderly woman in the usual peasant dress – white undergarment with long coloured double apron, front and back. When I came close, she bowed and said, "The Herr Englishman?" "Yes," I said, "Jonathan Harker." She smiled and gave some message to an elderly man in white shirt-sleeves who had followed her to the door. He went out but immediately returned with a letter:-

"My friend – Welcome to the Carpathians. I am anxiously expecting you. Sleep well tonight. At three tomorrow the coach will start for Bukovina; a place on it is kept for you. At the Borgo Pass my carriage will await you and will bring you to me. I trust that your journey from London has been a happy one, and that you will enjoy your stay in my beautiful land.

"Your friend,

"Dracula."

4 May. I found that my landlord had got a letter from the Count, telling him to secure the best place on the coach for me, but when I made a few inquiries about details, he did not answer and pretended he could not understand my German. This could not be true, because up to then he had understood it perfectly. He and his wife, the old lady who had received me, looked at each other in a frightened sort of way. He mumbled that some money had been sent in the letter and that was all he knew. When I asked him if he knew Count Dracula, and could tell me anything about his castle, both he and his wife crossed themselves and, saying they knew nothing at all, refused to say any more. This was all very mysterious and by no means comforting.

Just as I was leaving, the old lady came up to my room and said in a very hysterical way. "Must you go? Oh! young Herr, must you go?" When I told her I must go at once as I was engaged on important business, she asked again, "Do you know what day it is?" I answered that it was the fourth of May. She shook her head and said, "Oh yes, I know that, but do you know what day it is?" On my saying that I did not understand, she went on, "It is the eve of St George's Day. Do you not know that tonight, when the clock strikes midnight, all the evil things in the world will come to power? Do you know where you are going and what you are going to?"

She was in such evident distress that I tried to comfort her, but said again that I had to go. It was my duty. Then she dried her eyes and, taking a crucifix on a rosary from her neck, offered it to me. I did not know what to do, but did not wish to offend her. She saw, I suppose, the doubt on my face, for she put the rosary round my neck and said, "For your mother's sake," and went out of the room.

I am writing up this part of my diary while I am waiting for the coach which is, of course, late, and the crucifix is still round my neck. I am not feeling nearly as easy in my mind as usual. If this book should ever reach my darling Mina before I do, let it bring my goodbye, and goodbye to our future marriage. Here comes the coach!

5 May. The Castle. When I got on the coach, the driver had not taken his seat, and I saw him talking with the landlady. They were evidently talking of me, for every now and then they looked at me, and some of the people who were sitting on the bench outside the door came and listened, and then looked at me, most of them pityingly.

When we started, the crowd round the inn door, which had by this time swelled to a considerable size, all made the sign of the cross and pointed two fingers towards me. With some difficulty I got a fellow passenger to tell me what they meant; he would not answer at first, but on learning that I was English, he explained that it was a charm or guard against the evil eye. This was not very pleasant for me, just starting for an unknown place to meet an unknown man, but every one seemed so kind-hearted and so sorrowful and so sympathetic that I was greatly touched. I shall never forget the last glimpse which I had of the inn yard and its crowd of picturesque figures all crossing themselves, as they stood round the wide archway with its background of rich foliage of oleander and orange trees in green tubs clustered in the centre of the yard. Then our driver cracked his big whip over his four small horses which ran abreast, and we set off on our journey.

I soon forgot my ghostly fears in the beauty of the scene as we drove along. Before us lay a green sloping land full of forests and woods, with here and there steep hills, crowned with clumps of trees or with farmhouses, the blank gable end to the road. There was everywhere a bewildering mass of fruit blossom – apple, plum, pear, cherry; and as we drove by I could see the green grass under the trees spangled with the fallen petals. Beyond the green swelling hills rose mighty forests leading up to the height of the Carpathian mountains. Right and left of us they towered, with the afternoon sun falling full upon them and bringing out all the glorious colours of this beautiful range, deep blue and purple in the shadows of the peaks, green and brown where the grass and rock mingled, and as far as the eye could see, jagged rocks and pointed crags and behind and above them the snowy peaks rising grandly. Our road wound on and on and it began to grow dark and misty and the air grew cold. Sometimes the hills were so steep that, although our driver seemed to be in a hurry, the horses could only go slowly. I wished to get down and walk up the hills as we do at home, but the driver would not hear of it.

"No, no," he said, "you must not walk here. The dogs are too fierce."

The only stop he would make was a moment's pause to light his lamps. We appeared to fly along; the passengers appeared excited and the crazy coach rocked on its great leather springs, and swayed like a boat tossed on a stormy sea. I had to hold on. Then the mountains seemed to come nearer to us on each side and to frown down upon us. We were entering on the Borgo Pass. As we flew along, the driver leaned forward, and on each side the passengers, craning over the edge of the coach, peered eagerly into the darkness. At last we saw before us the Pass opening out on the eastern side. There were dark, rolling clouds overhead and in the air the heavy, oppressive sense of thunder. I was now myself looking out for the carriage which would be taking me to the Count. Each moment I expected to see the glare of the lamps through the blackness, but all was dark. The only light was the flickering rays of our own lamps, in which the steam from our hard-driven horses rose in a white cloud. We could see now the sandy road lying white before us, but there was on it no sign of a vehicle. I felt some disappointment, but the passengers drew back with a sigh of gladness which I could not understand. I was already thinking what I had best do, when the driver, looking at his watch, said quietly to the others, "We are early." Then turning to me, he said in German worse than my own, "There is no carriage here. You are not expected after all. We will now go on to Bukovina and return tomorrow or the next day, better the next day." While he was speaking, the horses began to neigh and snort and plunge wildly, so that the driver had to hold them up. The peasants began to scream and cross themselves and, at that moment, a carriage with four horses drove up behind us, overtook us and drew up beside the coach. I could see from the flash of our lamps, as the rays fell on them, that the horses were coal-black and splendid animals. They were driven by a tall man, with a long brown beard and a great, black hat, which seemed to hide his face from us. I could only see the gleam of a pair of very bright eyes, which seemed red in the lamplight, as he turned to us. He said to the driver, "You are early tonight, my friend."

"The gentleman was in a hurry," replied the driver, stammering and looking uncomfortable.

"That is why, I suppose, you wished him to go on to Bukovina. You cannot deceive me, my friend. I know too much, and my horses are swift." As he spoke, he smiled, and the lamplight fell on a hard-looking mouth, with very red lips and sharp-looking teeth, as white as ivory. One of my companions whispered to another something which sounded like, "The dead travel fast." The strange driver evidently heard the words, for he looked up with a gleaming smile. The passenger turned his face away and again made the sign of the cross. "Give me the gentleman's luggage," said the driver, and my bags were speedily handed out and put in the carriage. Then I got down from the side of the coach, as the carriage was close alongside, its driver helping me with a hand which caught my arm in a grip of steel. Without a word, he shook his reins, the horses turned, and we swept into the darkness of the Pass.

The carriage went at a hard pace straight along, then we made a complete turn and went along another straight road. It seemed to me that we were simply going over and over the same ground again, and so I took note of certain points and found that this was so. Presently I struck a match, and by its flame looked at my watch; it was within a few minutes of midnight. This gave me a sort of shock, and I waited with a sick feeling of suspense. Then a dog began to howl somewhere in a farmhouse far down the road – a long, agonized wailing as if from fear. The sound was taken up by another dog, and then another and another, till borne on the wind which now sighed softly through the Pass, a wild howling began which seemed to come from all over the country. At the first howl, the horses began to strain and rear, but the driver spoke to them soothingly, and they quietened down, but shivered and sweated as though they had run away from a sudden fright. Then far off in the distance, from the mountains on each side of us, began a louder and a sharper howling – that of wolves – which terrified both the horses and myself. I wanted to jump from the carriage and run while they reared again and plunged madly, so that the driver had to use all his great strength to stop them from bolting. In a few moments, however, my own ears got accustomed to the sound, and the horses became quiet enough for the driver to get down and stroke them and talk soothingly to them. Soon they became manageable again, though they still trembled. The driver again took his seat and, shaking his reins, started off at a great pace. This time, after going to the far side of the Pass, he suddenly turned down a narrow roadway which ran sharply to the right.

Soon we were hemmed in with trees, which in places arched right over the roadway, so that it seemed as if we were passing through a tunnel; and again, great frowning rocks guarded us boldly on either side. Though we were sheltered by the trees, we could hear the rising wind, for it moaned and whistled through the rocks, and the branches of the trees crashed together as we swept along. It grew colder and colder still, and fine, powdery snow began to fall, so that soon we and all around us were covered with a white blanket. The keen wind still carried the howling of the dogs, though this grew fainter as we went on our way. The baying of the wolves sounded nearer and nearer, as though they were closing round on us from every side. I grew dreadfully afraid, and the horses shared my fear. But I heard the driver's voice raised in a tone of imperious command, and he made a gesture with his arm, as though brushing aside an obstacle. At once the wolves fell back and troubled us no more.

The carriage was climbing now, sometimes going

downhill but mainly always climbing. Suddenly I became aware that the driver was pulling up the horses in the courtyard of a vast, ruined castle, from whose full black windows came no ray of light, and whose broken battlements showed a jagged line against a moonlit sky.

Chapter II

JONATHAN HARKER'S JOURNAL – CONTINUED

5 May. I must have been asleep, for certainly if I had been fully awake I would have noticed the approach of such a remarkable place. In the gloom, the courtyard looked of considerable size, and as several dark ways led from it under great round arches, it seemed bigger than it really is. I have not yet been able to see it by daylight.

When the coach stopped, the driver jumped down and held out his hand to assist me to alight. Then he took out my bags and placed them on the ground beside me as I stood close to a great door, old and studded with iron nails and set in a projecting doorway of massive carved stone. As I stood, the driver jumped again into his seat and shook the reins; the horses started forward, and trap and all disappeared down one of the dark openings.

I stood in silence where I was, for I did not know

what to do, and I felt doubts and fears crowding upon me. What sort of place had I come to, and among what kind of people? What sort of grim adventure was it on which I had embarked? This was not a usual incident in the life of a young, recently qualified solicitor sent out to explain the purchase of London estate to a foreigner.

In a minute or two I heard a heavy step approaching behind the great door, and saw through the chinks the gleam of a light. Then there was the sound of rattling chains and the clanking of massive bolts drawn back. A key was turned with a loud grating noise, and the great door swung back.

Within stood a tall old man, clean shaven except for a long white moustache, and clad in black from head to foot, without a single speck of colour about him anywhere. He held in his hand an old silver lamp in which the flame burned without a chimney or glass of any kind, throwing long quivering shadows as it flickered in the draught of the open door. The old man motioned me in with his right hand with a courtly gesture, saying in English, "Welcome to my house! Enter freely and of your own will!"

He did not come forward to meet me, but stood like a statue, as though he were made of stone. The instant, however, that I had stepped over the threshold, he moved quickly forward and, holding out his hand, grasped mine with a strength which made me wince. His hand was cold as ice – more like the hand of a dead than living man. Its strength was so like that of my driver, whose face I had not seen, that I thought it might be the same person to whom I was speaking, so to make sure I asked him if he was Count Dracula.

"I am Dracula," he replied, "and I bid you welcome. Come in, Mr Harker; the night air is chill and you must eat and rest." As he was speaking, he put the lamp on a bracket on the wall, and before I could prevent it, picked up my luggage. I protested but he insisted, "Nay sir, you are my guest. It is late and my people have retired for the night. Let me see to your comfort myself."

He insisted on carrying my bags along the passage and then up a great winding stair, and along another great passage, on whose stone floor our steps rang heavily. At the end of this he threw open a heavy door, and I rejoiced to see within a well-lit room in which a table was spread for supper, and on whose mighty hearth a great fire of logs flamed and flared. The Count halted, putting down my bags, closed the door and, crossing the room, opened another door, which led into a small octagonal room lit by a single lamp, and seemingly without a window of any sort. Passing through this, he opened another door, and invited me to enter. It was a welcome sight, for here was a great bedroom well-lighted and warmed with another log fire which sent a hollow roar up the wide chimney. The Count himself left my luggage inside and withdrew, saying, before he closed the doors, "You will need, after your journey, to wash and refresh yourself. I trust you will find all you wish. When you are ready, come into the other room, where you will find your supper prepared."

The light and warmth and the Count's courteous welcome reassured me somewhat. I was half-famished with hunger, so, after a hasty wash, I went into the other room.

I found supper already laid out. My host, who stood on one side of the great fireplace, leaning against the stonework, made a graceful wave of his hand to the table and said, "I pray you, be seated and sup how you please. You will, I trust, excuse me that I do not join you, but I have dined already."

I handed to him the sealed letter which Mr Hawkins, my employer, had entrusted to me. He opened it and read it gravely, then, with a charming smile, handed it to me to read. The letter explained that the writer was crippled with gout and unable to travel. He was sending me with every confidence to attend on the Count and take his instructions.

The Count himself came forward and took off the cover of a dish, and I fell to at once on an excellent roast chicken. This, with some cheese and salad and a bottle of old Tokay, a famous Hungarian wine, of which I had two glasses, was my supper. During the time I was eating it, the Count asked me many questions as to my journey, and I told him by degrees all I had experienced.

By this time I had finished my supper and had drawn up a chair by the fire and begun to smoke a cigar which he offered me, at the same time telling me that he did not smoke. I now had an opportunity of observing him closely.

He had a high-bridged, thin nose with peculiarly arched nostrils, a lofty domed forehead, little hair on the temples but a great deal elsewhere. His eyebrows were very massive, almost meeting over the nose. They were bushy and curling. The mouth, so far as I could see it under the heavy moustache, was fixed and rather cruel-looking, with peculiarly sharp white teeth. They protruded over his lips which were remarkably red for a man of his years. His ears were pale, and at the tops extremely pointed, the chin was broad and strong, and the cheeks firm though thin. He looked to me extremely pale.

I had noticed the backs of his hands before as they lay on his knees in the firelight, and they had seemed rather white and fine, but seeing them close to me, I could not help noticing that they were rather coarse – broad with squat fingers. Strange to say, there were hairs in the centre of the palm. The nails were long and fine, and cut to a sharp point. As the Count leaned over me and his hands touched me, I could not help shuddering, and a feeling of sickness came over me. The Count, evidently noticing this, drew back, and with a grim sort of smile, which showed more than he had yet done of his sharp teeth, sat himself down again on his own side of the fireplace. We were both silent for a while, and as I looked towards the window I saw the first dim streak of the coming dawn. There seemed a strange stillness over everything, but, as I listened, I heard as if from down below in the valley, the howling of many wolves. The Count's eyes gleamed and he said, "Listen to them – the children of the night. What music they make!" Seeing, I suppose, a strange expression on my face, he added, "Ah, sir, you dwellers in the city cannot enter into the feelings of the hunter." Then he rose and said, "But you must be tired. Your bedroom is all ready, and tomorrow you shall sleep as late as you wish. I will have to be away till the afternoon, so sleep well and dream well!" With a courteous bow, he opened for me himself the door to the octagonal room, and I entered my bedroom . . .

I am all in a sea of wonders. I doubt; I fear; I think strange things, which I dare not confess to my own soul. Good keep me, if only for the sake of those dear to me!

7 May. It is again early morning, but I have rested and have enjoyed the last twenty-four hours. I slept till late in the day, and awoke of my own accord. When I had dressed myself, I went into the room where we had supped, and found a cold breakfast laid out, with coffee kept hot by the pot being placed on the hearth. There was a card on the table, on which was written, "I have to be absent for a while. Do not wait for me. D." I set to and enjoyed a hearty meal. When I had done, I looked for a bell, so that I might let the servants know I had finished, but I could not find one. In spite of the beautiful furnishings and signs of great wealth, there are some things lacking. In none of the rooms is there a mirror, not even in my bedroom, so that I had to get a little shaving glass from my bag before I could either shave or brush my hair. I have not yet seen a servant anywhere, or heard a sound near the castle except the howling of wolves.

Some time after I had finished my meal – I do not know whether to call it breakfast or dinner, for it was between five and six o'clock when I had it – I looked about for something to read, for I did not like to go about the castle until I had asked the Count's permission. There was absolutely nothing in my room, book, newspaper, or even writing materials, so I opened another door in the room and found a sort of library. The door opposite mine I tried, but found it locked.

In the library I found, to my great delight, a vast number of English books, whole shelves full of them, and bound volumes of magazines and newspapers. There were also reference books, and a table in the centre was littered with English magazines and newspapers, though none of them were of very recent date.

While I was looking at the books, the door opened, and the Count entered. He greeted me in a hearty way, and hoped that I had had a good night's rest. Then he went on:

"I am glad you found your way here, for I am sure there is much that will interest you. These companions" – and he laid his hand on some of the books – "have been good friends to me, and for some years past, ever since I had the idea of going to London, have given me many, many hours of pleasure. Through them I have come to know your great England, and to know her is to love her. I can read the books, but do not, as yet, speak English well."

"But Count," I said, "you speak excellently."

He bowed and said, "You come to me not only as agent of my friend Peter Hawkins, of Exeter, to tell me all about my new estate in London. You shall, I trust, stay here with me awhile and help me to master your language. I am sorry that I had to be away so long today, but you will I know forgive me. I have many important affairs in hand."

Of course I said I understood and asked if I might come into the room when I chose. He answered, "Yes, certainly," and added, "You may go anywhere you wish in the castle, except where the doors are locked, where of course you will not wish to go. There are reasons for things to be as they are, and if you could see with my eyes and know what I know, you could perhaps better understand." I said I was sure of that and then he went on, "We are in Transylvania, and Transylvania is not England. Our ways are not your ways, and you will see and hear many strange things. Indeed, from what you have told me of your experiences, you know something already of what strange things there may be; but come, tell me of London and of the house which you have procured for me."

With an apology for not having produced the information before, I went into my room to get the papers from my bag. While I was placing them in order, I heard a rattling of china and silver in the next room, and as I passed through, I noticed that the table had been cleared and the lamp lit, for it was by this time deep into the dark. The lamps were also lit in the study or library, and I found the Count lying on the sofa reading. When I came in, he cleared the books and papers from the table, and with him I went into plans and deeds and figures of all sorts. He was interested in everything and asked me a myriad questions about the place and its surroundings. He had evidently studied everything he could get about the neighbourhood, and it was evident that he knew very much more than I did. We went thoroughly into the business of the purchase of the estate at Purfleet near London. When I had told him the facts and got his signature to the necessary papers, and had written a letter with them ready to post to Mr Hawkins, he began to ask me more about Carfax, the house he was buying.

I told him it was old, surrounded by a high wall and in a bad state of repair. It was set in grounds of some twenty acres with many trees, which made it in places gloomy, and there was a deep, dark-looking pond or small lake evidently fed by some springs, as the water was clear and flowed away in a fair-sized stream. The house was very large and looked as if it had once been part of a castle keep. Close by was an old chapel or church which I had not been able to enter as I did not have the key of the door leading to it from the house.

When I had finished, he said, "I am glad that it is old and big. I myself am of an old family, and to live in a new house would kill me. I rejoice also that there is a chapel of old times. We Transylvanian nobles love to know that our bones may not lie among the common dead."

Presently, with an excuse, he left me, asking me to put all my papers together. It was the better part of an hour when he returned saying, "Come, I am informed that your supper is ready." He took my arm and we went into the next room, where I found an excellent supper ready on the table. He told me that he had already dined out, but he sat as on the previous night, and chatted while I ate. After supper I smoked, as on the last evening, and the Count stayed with me, chatting and asking questions hour after hour. I was not sleepy but could not help feeling that chill which comes over one at the coming of the dawn, which is like, in its way, the turn of the tide. They say that people who are near death die generally at dawn or at the turn of the tide. All at once we heard the crow of the cock through the clear morning air. Count Dracula, jumping to his feet, said, "Why, there is the morning again! How thoughtless of me to let you stay up so long. You must make your conversation about my dear new country of England less interesting, so that I may not forget how time flies by us," and, with a courtly bow, he quickly left me.

I went into my own room and drew the curtains, but there was little to see; my window opened on to the courtyard and all I could see was the warm grey of the dawn. So I pulled the curtains again and have written of this day.

8 May. I began to fear as I wrote in this book that I was going into too much detail about everything, but now I am glad I did, for there is something so strange about this place that I feel uneasy. I wish I were safe out of it, or that I had never come. If there were anyone to talk to, I could bear it, but there is only the Count.

I only slept a few hours when I went to bed, and, feeling that I could not sleep any more, I got up. I had hung my shaving glass by the window and was just beginning to shave. Suddenly I felt a hand on my shoulder, and heard the Count's voice saying to me, "Good morning." I started, for it amazed me that I had not seen him, since the reflection of the glass covered the whole room behind me. In starting, I had cut myself slightly, but I did not notice it at the moment. Having answered the Count's greeting, I turned to the glass again to see if I had been mistaken. This time there was no doubt about it, for the man was close to me, and I could see him over my shoulder, but there was no reflection of him in the mirror! The whole room behind me was displayed, but there was no sign of a man in it, except myself. This was startling, and, coming on the top of so many strange things, was beginning to increase that vague uneasiness which I always have when the Count is near; but at that moment I realized that my cut had bled a little and the blood was trickling over my chin. I laid down the razor, turning as I did so half round to look for some sticking plaster. When the Count saw my face, his eyes blazed with a sort of devilish fury, and he suddenly made a grab at my throat. I drew away, and his hand touched the string of beads which held the crucifix. It made an instant change in him, for his fury passed so quickly that I could hardly believe it had ever been there.

"Take care," he said, "take care how you cut yourself. It is more dangerous than you think in this country." Then, seizing the shaving glass, he went on, "And this is the wretched thing that has done the mischief. Away with it!" And opening the heavy window with one wrench of his terrible hand, he flung out my shaving glass, which was shattered into a thousand pieces on the stones of the courtyard far below. Then, without a word, he left the room. It is very annoying, for shaving now will be even more difficult than it was before.

When I went into the dining-room, breakfast was prepared, but I could not find the Count anywhere, so I breakfasted alone. It is strange that so far I had not seen the Count eat or drink. He must be a very peculiar man. After breakfast I did a little exploring in the castle. I went out on the stairs, and found a room looking towards the South. The view was magnificent. The castle is on the very edge of a terrible precipice. A stone falling from the window would fall a thousand feet without touching anything! As far as the eye can reach there is a sea of green tree tops, with occasionally a deep rift where there is a chasm. Here and there are silver threads where the rivers wind in deep gorges through the forests.

But I have no heart to describe beauty, for when I had seen the view, I explored further; doors, doors, doors everywhere, and all locked and bolted. One could get out of the castle only through one of the windows. The castle is a prison, and I am a prisoner!

Chapter III

JONATHAN HARKER'S JOURNAL – CONTINUED

When I found that I was a prisoner, a sort of wild feeling came over me. I rushed up and down stairs trying every door and peering out of every window I could find, but, after a while, I realized I was completely helpless. I was like a rat in a trap. I sat down and thought about it and decided to keep my fears to myself and my eyes open.

I had hardly come to this conclusion when I heard the great door below shut, and knew that the Count had returned. He did not come at once into the library, so I went cautiously to my own room and found him making the bed. This was odd, but only confirmed what I had all along thought – that there were no servants in the house. When later I saw him through the chink of the hinges laying the table in the dining-room, I was certain, for if he himself performs such tasks, surely it is proof that there is no one else to do them. This gave me a fright, for if there is no one else in the castle, it must have been the Count himself who was the driver of the coach that brought me here. This is a terrible thought; for if so, what does it mean that he could control the wolves, as he did, by only holding up his hand. How was it that all the people at Bistritz and on the coach had some terrible fear for me? Bless that good, good woman who hung the crucifix round my neck, for it is a comfort and a strength to me whenever I touch it. In the meantime I must find out all I can about Count Dracula, as it may help me to understand. Tonight he may talk of himself, if I turn the conversation that way. I must be very careful, however, not to arouse his suspicion.

Midnight. I have had a long talk with the Count. I asked him about the history of his country of which he is immensely proud. In speaking of people and things and especially battles, he spoke as if he had been present at them all, defending the honour of his noble house and family. He spoke at length and told me of his pride that he bore the ancient name of Dracula. When he had finished his tale, it was close on morning, and we went to bed. This diary seems horribly like the beginning of the "Arabian Nights", for everything has to break off at cockcrow.

12 May. Last evening, when the Count came from his room, he began by asking me questions on legal matters and on the doing of certain kinds of business. He particularly wished to know if he could arrange the shipping of his goods himself without going through his solicitor. He also explained why he had chosen solicitors as far away as Exeter to purchase a place for him near London. It was so that there could be no possible local knowledge of his affairs. For a man who had never been in my country, and who did not evidently do much in the way of business, his knowledge and keen wits were wonderful.

When he had satisfied himself on all the points he had raised, and I had checked them as well as I could by the books I had with me, he suddenly stood up and said, "Have you written to our friend Mr Peter Hawkins, or to any other?" It was with some bitterness in my heart that I answered that I had not, that as yet I had not had any opportunity of sending letters to anybody.

"Then write now, my young friend," he said, laying a heavy hand on my shoulder. "Write to our friend and to anyone else you wish and say, please, that you shall stay with me until a month from now."

"Do you wish me to stay so long?" I asked, for my heart grew cold at the thought.

"Yes, I desire it and will take no refusal. When your employer promised to send someone on his behalf, it was understood that I should decide the length of his stay. I have looked after you well. Is that not so?"

What could I do but agree? I had to think of Mr Hawkins, not myself, and besides, while Count Dracula was speaking, there was something in his eyes and in his manner which made me remember that I was a prisoner and that, in any case, I could have no choice. The Count saw his victory in my bow to him and his mastery in my troubled face, for he began at once to instruct me in his smooth, resistless way:

"I pray you, my good young friend, that you will not write of anything but business in your letters." As he spoke, he handed me three sheets of notepaper and three envelopes. They were the thinnest possible, and looking at them, then at him, and noticing his quiet smile, with the sharp teeth lying over the red underlip, I understood as well as if he had spoken that I should be careful what I wrote, for he would be able to read it.

So I decided to write only formal business notes now, but to write fully to Mr Hawkins in secret, and also to Mina, for to her I could write in shorthand, which would puzzle the Count, if he did see it. When I had written my letters, I sat quiet, reading a book while the Count wrote several notes, referring as he wrote them to some books on his table. Then he took up my two and placed them with his own, and put by his writing materials, after which, the instant the door had closed behind him, I leaned over and looked at the letters, which were face down on the table. I felt it was not wrong to do this, for I must protect myself in every way I could.

One of the letters was directed to a man named Billington in Whitby, another to a Herr Leutner in a place called Varna, the third was to a London bank and the fourth to a bank in Budapest. The second and fourth letters were unsealed. I was about to look at them when I saw the door-handle move. I sank back in my chair, having just had time to replace the letters as they had been and to resume my book before the Count, holding still another letter in his hand, entered the room. He took up the letters on the table and stamped them carefully, and then turning to me, said, "I trust you will forgive me, but I have much work to do in private this evening. You will, I hope, find all things as you wish." At the door he turned, and after a moment's pause said, "Let me warn you, my dear young friend, if you leave these rooms, not by any chance to go to sleep in any other part of the castle. It is old, and has many memories, and there are bad dreams for those who sleep unwisely. If you are not careful about this, then – " He finished his speech in a gruesome way, for he motioned with his hands as if he were washing them. I quite understood; my only doubt was as to whether any dream could be more terrible than the unnatural, horrible net of gloom and mystery which seemed closing around me.

Later. I meant the last words written, but this time there is no doubt in question. I shall not fear to sleep in any place where is he not. I have placed the crucifix over the head of my bed – I imagine that my rest is thus freer from dreams – and there it shall remain.

When he left me, I went to my room. After a little while, not hearing any sound, I came out and went up the stone stairs to where I could look out towards the South. Looking out on the vast space instead of the narrow darkness of the courtyard, I felt the need of fresh air. I gazed out over the beautiful expanse, bathed in soft yellow moonlight till it was almost as light as day. In the soft light the distant hills seemed melted, and the shadows in the valleys and gorges of a velvety blackness. Its beauty seemed to cheer me; there was peace and comfort in every breath I drew. As I leaned from the window, my eye was caught by something moving below me, and somewhat to my left, where I imagined, from the way the rooms were arranged, that the windows of the Count's own room would look out. The window at which I stood was tall and deep. I drew back behind the stonework, and looked carefully out.

What I saw was the Count's head coming out from the window. I did not see the face, but I knew the man by the neck and the movement of his back and arms. In any case I could not mistake the hands which I had looked at so often. I was at first interested and somewhat amused, for it is wonderful how small a matter will interest and amuse a man when he is a prisoner. But my feelings changed to repulsion and terror when I saw the whole man slowly emerge from the window and begin to crawl down the castle wall over that dreadful abyss, *face down*, with his cloak spreading out around him like great wings. I saw his fingers and toes grasp the corners of the stones where the mortar had been worn away, and in this way he moved downwards with considerable speed, just as a lizard moves along a wall. Is this a man or a creature looking like a man? I am filled with the dread of this horrible place. I am in awful fear and there is no escape for me. I am surrounded with terrors that I dare not think of . . .

15 May. Once more I have seen the Count go out in his lizard fashion. He moved downwards in a sidelong way, some hundred feet down, and a good deal to the left. He vanished into some hole or window. When his head had disappeared, I leaned out to try and see more, but found that the distance was too great to allow a proper angle of sight. I knew he had left the castle now, and decided to explore. I went back to my room and, taking a lamp, tried all the doors. They were all locked, as I had expected, and the locks were fairly new, but I went down the stone stairs to the hall where I had first entered. I found that I could pull back the bolts easily enough and unhook the great chains, but the door was locked and the key was gone! That key must be in the Count's room. I must watch to see if his door is ever unlocked so that I may get it and escape. I went on to explore the stairs and passages and to try the doors that opened from them. At last I found one door at the top of a stairway which, though it seemed to be locked, gave way when I pushed it. I pushed harder and found that the hinges had fallen and that the heavy door was resting on the floor. With great effort I forced it back and entered. I was now in a wing of the castle further to the right, and lower than the rooms I knew.

I was evidently in a part of the castle occupied by the ladies in bygone days. The furniture, though covered in dust, had more of an air of comfort that any I had seen elsewhere in the castle. My lamp had little effect in the brilliant moonlight which came from the windows, but I was glad to have it with me, for there was a dread loneliness in the place which chilled my heart and made my nerves tremble. Still, it was better than living alone in the rooms which I had begun to hate from the presence of the Count, and presently I found a sense of quietness coming over me. Here I am, sitting at a little oak table where in old times perhaps a fair lady sat to write to her loved one, and writing in my diary in shorthand all that has happened since I closed it last.

Later: the Morning of 16 May. May God preserve me from going mad! When I had written in my diary and had fortunately replaced the book and pen in my pocket, I felt sleepy. The Count's warning came into my mind, but I took a pleasure in disobeying it. I decided not to return tonight to the gloom-haunted rooms, but to sleep here where ladies of old had sat and sung and lived sweet lives and mourned for their menfolk away at the wars. I drew a great couch out of its place near the corner, so that as I lay I could look at the lovely view to east and south, and caring nothing for the dust composed myself for sleep. I suppose I must have fallen asleep, but I am not sure, for all that followed was startlingly real.

I was not alone. In the moonlight opposite me were three young women but, though the moonlight was behind them, they threw no shadow on the floor. They came close to me and looked at me for some time, and then whispered together. Two were dark and had a likeness to the count, and great, dark piercing eyes that seemed to be almost red when contrasted with the pale yellow moon. The other was fair, as fair can be, with great wavy masses of golden hair and eyes like pale sapphires. All three had brilliant white teeth that shone like pearls against the ruby of their lips. There was something about them that made me uneasy – some longing and at the same time some deadly fear. I desired that they would kiss me with those red lips. I do not like writing this down, for Mina might read it and it would cause her pain, but it is the truth. They whispered together and then they all three laughed – such a silvery, musical laugh, but as hard as though the sound never could have come through the softness of human lips. The fair girl shook her head, and the other two urged her on. One said, "Go on! You are first and we shall follow; yours is the right to begin." The other added, "He is young and strong; there are kisses for us all." I lay quiet, looking out from under my eyelashes, and waited in an agony of delight. The fair girl advanced and bent over me until I could feel the movement of her breath upon me. Then she went on her knees and bent over me, gloating, and as she arched her neck, she actually licked her lips like an animal. Lower and lower went her head as her lips went below my mouth and chin and seemed about to fasten on my throat. I could feel the soft, shivering touch of the lips on the sensitive skin of my throat, and the hard dents of two sharp teeth, just touching and pausing there. I closed my eyes and waited, with a beating heart.

But at that instant another sensation swept through me as quick as lightning. I realized the Count was there, and he was lapped in a storm of fury. As I opened my eyes, I saw his strong hand grasp the slender neck of the fair woman and, with the power of a giant, draw it back. Her blue eyes were transformed with fury, the white teeth champed with rage, and the fair cheeks were blazing red with passion. But the Count! His eyes burned red as if the flames of hell-fire blazed behind them, and his face was deathly pale. With a fierce sweep of his arm, he hurled the woman from him and

have never been used; what furniture there was was covered in dust. I looked for the key, but it was not in the lock, and I could not find it anywhere. The only thing I found was a great heap of gold in one corner – gold of all kinds, Roman, and British, and Austrian, and Hungarian, and Greek and Turkish money, covered with a film of dust, as though it had lain long in the ground. None of it was less than three hundred years old. There were also chains and ornaments, some jewelled, but all of them old and stained.

At one corner of the room was a heavy door. I tried it for, since I could not find the key of the room or the key of the outer door, which was the main object of my search, I must continue exploring or all my efforts would be in vain. It was open, and led through a stone passage to a circular stairway, which went steeply down. I descended, minding carefully where I went, for the stairs were dark, being lit only by loopholes in the heavy masonry. At the bottom I went down a passage, and at last I pulled open a heavy door which stood ajar and found myself in an old, ruined chapel, which had evidently been used as a graveyard. The roof was broken, and in two places were steps leading to vaults, but the ground had recently been dug over and placed in great wooden boxes, obviously those which had been brought by the Slovaks. There was nobody about. Overcoming my fear, I went down into the vaults. I went into two but saw nothing except fragments of old coffins and piles of dust; in the third, however, I made a discovery.

There, in one of the great boxes, of which there were fifty in all, on a pile of newly dug earth, lay the Count! He was either dead or asleep; I could not say which, for there seemed to be no pulse, no breath, no beating of the heart. By the side of the box was its cover, pierced with holes here and there. Not stopping to look for his keys, I fled from the place, and leaving the Count's room by the window, crawled again up the castle wall. Regaining my room, I threw myself panting upon the bed and tried to think . . .

29 June. Today is the date of my last letter, and the Count has taken steps to prove that it was genuine, for again I saw him leave the castle by the same window, and in my clothes. As he went down the wall, lizard fashion, I wished I had a gun so that I might destroy him, but I fear that no weapon made by man would have any effect on him. I dared not wait to see him return, for I feared to see those weird sisters again. I came back to the library and read there till I fell asleep.

I was awakened by the Count who looked at me grimly and said, "Tomorrow, my friend, we must part. You return to your beautiful England, and I to my work. Your letter home has been despatched; tomorrow I shall not be here, but all shall be ready for your journey. In the morning the gypsies come and have some labours of their own here, and, too, some Slovaks will come. When they have gone, my carriage will come for you, and shall bear you to the Borgo Pass to meet the coach from Bukovina to Bistritz. But I am in hopes that I shall see more of you at Castle Dracula." I suspected him, and made up my mind to test him, so I asked him straight out, "Why may I not go tonight?"

"Because, dear sir, my coachman and horses are away on a mission."

"But I would walk with pleasure. I want to get away at once." He smiled, such a soft, smooth, diabolical smile that I knew there was some trick behind his smoothness.

"And your baggage?"

"I do not care about it. I can send for it some other time."

The Count stood up and said sweetly, "Come with me, my dear young friend. Not an hour shall you wait in my house against your will, though I am sad at your going, and that you so suddenly desire it. Come then."

Carrying the lamp, he went before me down the stairs and along the hall. Suddenly he stopped. "Hark!" Close at hand came the howling of many wolves. It was almost as if the sound sprang up at the raising of his hand. After a moment's pause, he went to the door, drew back the bolts, unhooked the heavy chains, and began to draw it open.

To my intense astonishment, I saw that it was unlocked. Suspiciously, I looked all round but could see no key of any kind.

As the door began to open, the howling of the wolves outside grew louder and angrier; their red jaws, with champing teeth, and their blunt-clawed feet as they leaped, came in through the opening door. I knew then that to struggle at the moment against the Count was useless. With such allies as these at his command, I could do nothing. But still the door continued slowly to open, and only the Count's body stood in the gap. Suddenly it struck me that I was to be given to the wolves, and that this might be the moment of my doom. I cried out, "Shut the door; I shall wait till morning!" and covered my face with my hands to hide my tears of bitter disappointment. With one sweep of his powerful arm, the Count threw the door shut, and great bolts clanged and echoed through the hall as they shot back into their places.

In silence we returned to the library, and after a minute or two I went to my room. The last I saw of Count Dracula was his kissing his hand to me with a red light of triumph in his eyes and the smile of the devil himself.

When I was in my room and about to lie down, I

thought I heard a whispering at my door. I went to it softly and listened. I thought I heard the voice of the Count: "Back, back, to your own place! Your time is not yet come. Wait! Have patience! Tonight is mine. Tomorrow night is yours!" There was a low, sweet ripple of laughter, and in a rage I threw open the door, and saw outside the three terrible women licking their lips. As I appeared, they all joined in a horrible laugh, and ran away.

I came back to my room and threw myself on my knees. Is it then so near the end? Tomorrow! Tomorrow! Lord, help me, and those to whom I am dear!

30 June. Morning. These may be the last words I ever write in this diary. I slept until just before dawn, and when I woke, threw myself on my knees, for I am determined that if Death comes, he shall find me ready.

At last I felt a change in the air and knew that the morning had come. Then came the welcome cockcrow, and I felt that I was safe. With a glad heart, I took my rosary and crucifix, opened my door and ran down to the hall. I had seen that the door was unlocked, and now escape was before me. With hands that trembled with eagerness, I unhooked the chains and drew back the massive bolts.

But the door would not move. Despair seized me. I pulled and pulled at the door, and shook it till, massive as it was, it rattled in its casement. I could see that the bolt was shot. It had been locked after I left the Count.

I decided to obtain the key at any risk. I would scale the wall again and get into the Count's room. He might kill me, but I must do it. Without a pause, I rushed up to the East window, and scrambled down the wall as before into the Count's room. It was empty, but I had rather expected this. I could not see a key anywhere, but the heap of gold remained. I went through the door in the corner and down the winding stair and along the dark passage to the old chapel. I knew now well enough where to find the monster I sought.

The great box was in the same place, close against the wall, but the lid was laid on it, not fastened down, but with the nails ready in their places to be hammered home. I knew I must reach the body for the key, so I raised the lid and laid it back against the wall. There lay the Count. He looked younger. The hair and moustache were now a dark iron-grey; the cheeks were fatter, and the white skin seemed ruby-red underneath. The mouth was redder than ever, for on the lips were gouts of fresh blood, which trickled from the corner of the mouth and ran over the chin and neck. It seemed as if the whole awful creature were gorged in blood, and I shuddered as I bent over him, but I had to search or I was lost. I felt all over the body, but no sign could I find of the key. What should I do now?

As I though desperately of my next move, I heard in the distance a gypsy song sung by merry voices coming closer, and through their song the rolling heavy wheels and the cracking of whips; the gypsies and Slovaks of whom the Count had spoken were coming. I ran from the vault to the Count's room, determined to rush out the moment the door was opened. With strained ears I listened and heard downstairs the grinding of the key in the great lock and the falling back of the heavy door. Someone had a second key. At that moment there came a gust of wind and the old door of the Count's room blew shut with a shock that sent the dust flying. When I ran to push it open, I found that it was hopelessly fast. I was again a prisoner and the net of doom was closing round me.

As I write there is in the passage below a sound of many tramping feet and the crash of weights being set down heavily, most likely the boxes with their cargo of earth. There is a sound of hammering; it is the box being nailed down. Now I can hear the heavy feet tramping again along the hall, with other feet coming behind them.

The door is shut, and the chains rattle; there is a grinding of the key in the lock. I can hear the key withdraw. Then another door opens and shuts. I hear the creaking of lock and bolt. Hark! In the courtyard and down the rocky way comes the roll of heavy wheels, the crack of whips and the chorus of the gypsies as they pass into the distance.

I am alone in the castle with those awful women! I shall not remain alone with them. There remains still the window. I shall try to scale the castle wall, farther than I have yet attempted. I shall take some of the gold with me in case I want it later. I *shall* find a way from this dreadful place.

And then away for home! Away from this cursed spot, from this cursed land, where the devil and his children still walk with earthly feet. I throw myself on God's mercy. The precipice is steep and high. At its foot a man may sleep – as a man. Goodbye, Mina!

Chapter IV

Letter from Miss Mina Murray to Miss Lucy Westenra

9 May

My dearest Lucy,

Forgive my long delay in writing, but I have been simply overwhelmed with work. The life of an assistant schoolmistress is not easy. I am longing to be with you, and by the sea, where we can talk together freely and build our castles in the air. I have been working very hard lately, because I want to keep up with Jonathan's studies, and I have also been practising shorthand. When we are married, I shall be able to be useful to Jonathan and, if I am good enough at it, I can take down what he says and type it out for him. I am practising very hard at that as well. He and I sometimes write letters to each other in shorthand, and he is keeping a journal of his travels abroad in this way.

When I am with you, I shall keep a diary in shorthand. I shall try to do what I see journalists do: interviewing people and writing descriptions and trying to remember conversations.

I have just had a few hurried lines from Jonathan from Transylvania. He is well and will be returning in about a week. I am longing to hear his news. There is the ten o'clock bell ringing.

Good-bye
Your loving,
Mina

Tell me all the news when you write. You have not told me anything for a long time. I hear rumours, and especially of a tall, handsome, curly-haired man!

Letter from Lucy Westenra to Mina Murray

17 Chatham Street.
Wednesday.

My dearest Mina,

Who has been telling tales? The man you mention is Mr Arthur Holmwood. He often comes to see us, and he and Mama get on very well together. He has a Texan friend, a Mr Quincey Morris, who also seems to enjoy coming, but Arthur comes alone quite often.

We have also met a very clever doctor called John Seward. He is only twenty-nine, but is in charge of an immense lunatic asylum in Purfleet and has a house attached to the hospital. He comes often and says I have an interesting face. I think he is one of the most resolute men I ever saw, and yet the most calm. I can fancy what a wonderful power he must have over his patients. He would be just right for you if you were not already engaged to Jonathan!

All three of them seem to like coming to see me, but Mina, I must tell you, it is Arthur I love. I *think* he loves me, but he has not told me so in words. Write and tell me all you think about it, but keep it a secret between us. Good night. Bless me in your prayers and, dearest, pray for my happiness.

Lucy.

Letter from Lucy Westenra to Mina Murray

24 May.

My dearest Mina,

Thanks and thanks again for your sweet letter. It was so nice to be able to tell you and have your sympathy. It never rains but it pours. Here I am who will be twenty in September, and yet I never had a proposal till today – not a real proposal – and today I have had three: one from the doctor, one from Mr Morris and one from Arthur! I feel really and truly sorry for two of the poor fellows, but you will guess that I am now engaged to Arthur and I am so happy I don't know what to do with myself.

Dr Seward is a fine, strong man and, when I told him there was someone else, he took both my hands in his and said he hoped I would be happy, and that, if ever I wanted a friend, I must call on him. Mr Morris said much the same, and I felt that both would be good people to have as friends, especially in time of trouble. All three men know each other well and, although two are a little sad at the moment, they are pleased for Arthur and me. I am so happy. Must stop here for the moment.

Evening

Arthur has just gone, and I feel in better spirits than when I left off because, although it is Arthur I love, I feel so much for the other two. I am very, very happy and I don't know what I have done to deserve it. I must only try in future to show that I am grateful to God for all His goodness to me in sending to me such a lover, such a husband, and such a friend. Goodbye.

Ever your loving
Lucy.

MINA MURRAY'S JOURNAL

24 July. Whitby. Lucy met me at the station, looking sweeter and lovelier than ever, and we drove up to the house at the Crescent where she and her mother have rooms. This is a beautiful place, and I am glad to be with them, for I am worried about Jonathan. I had not heard from him for some time until, just before I came here, dear Mr Hawkins, who is always so kind, sent me a letter from him which he had just received. It is only a line sent from Castle Dracula, and it tells Mr Hawkins that Jonathan is just starting for home. That is not like Jonathan. I do not understand it, and it makes me uneasy.

27 July. I am still worried about Jonathan and now about Lucy as well. Although she looks so well, she has lately taken to her old habit of walking in her sleep. Her mother has spoken to me about it, and we have decided that I will lock the door of the room which we share every night.

3 August. Lucy continues to move about at night, and still no news from Jonathan, not even to Mr Hawkins, from whom I have just heard. I do hope he is not ill. He surely would have written. I look at that last letter of his, but somehow it does not satisfy me. It does not read like him, and yet it is his writing. There is no mistake about that. Lucy has not walked in her sleep much this week, but there is an odd look about her which I do not understand; even in her sleep, she seems to be watching me. She tries the door and, finding it locked, goes about the room searching for the key.

6 August. Another three days and no news. This suspense is getting dreadful. If only I knew where to write to or where to go to, I should feel easier, but no one has heard a word of Jonathan since that last letter. I must pray for patience. Lucy is more restless than ever, but is otherwise well.

Last night was very threatening, and the fishermen say we are in for a storm. The sea is tumbling in over the shallows and the sandy flats with a roar, muffled in the sea mists drifting inland. The horizon is lost in a grey mist. The fishing boats are racing for home, and rise and dip in the ground swell as they sweep into the harbour.

Presently the coastguard came along with his spyglass under his arm. He stopped to talk with me as he always does as I sit by the sea wall, but all the time he kept looking at a strange ship.

"I can't make her out," he said. "She's a Russian by the look of her, but she's knocking about in the queerest way. She seems to see the storm coming, but can't decide whether to run up north in the open, or to put in here. She is steered mighty strangely, if steered at all; changes about with every puff of wind. We'll hear more of her before this time tomorrow."

Chapter V

Cutting from The Daily Graph, *8 August,*
pasted into Mina Murray's Journal

From a Correspondent. Whitby.

One of the greatest and suddenest storms on record has just been experienced here, with results both strange and unique. The signs were there in the sky, the wind had dropped, and at midnight there was a dead calm, a sultry heat and a feel of thunder in the air. There were few lights in sight at sea, for even the coasting steamers, which usually hug the shore so closely, kept well to seaward, and few fishing boats were in sight. The only sail noticeable was a foreign schooner with all sails set, which seemed to be going westwards. All commented on the foolhardiness or ignorance of her officers, and efforts were made to signal her to reduce sail in face of her danger. Before night came down, she was seen with sails idly flapping as she gently rolled on the swell of the sea.

Then, without warning, the tempest broke. The waves rose in growing fury till in a very few minutes the sea was like a devouring monster. The wind roared like thunder and blew with such force that even strong men found it hard to keep their feet. The piers were cleared of onlookers, and a grim sea fog came drifting inland – white, wet clouds which swept by in ghostly fashion, so that the spirits of those lost at sea seemed to be touching their living brethren with the clammy hands of death, and many a one shuddered as the wreaths of sea mist swept by. At times the mist cleared, and the sea for some distance could be seen in the glare of the lightning, which now came thick and fast, followed by such sudden peals of thunder that the whole sky overhead seemed trembling under the shock of the footsteps of the storm.

On the summit of the East Cliff, the new searchlight was ready to be tried out. The officers in charge of it got it into working order and, whenever the mist lifted, swept its light across the surface of the sea. Once or twice a fishing boat, almost under water, rushed into harbour, able by the guidance of the light to avoid the danger of dashing against the piers. As each boat achieved the safety of the port, there was a shout of joy from the mass of people on the shore, which, in a moment, was swept away in the rush of the gale.

Before long the searchlight discovered some distance away a schooner with all sails set, apparently the same vessel which had been noticed earlier in the evening. The wind had by this time backed to the east, and there was a shudder among the watchers on the cliff as they realized the terrible danger in which she now was. Between her and the harbour lay the great flat reef on which so many good ships have suffered, and with the wind blowing from its present direction, it would be quite impossible for her to reach the entrance. Then the wind suddenly shifted to the North-East, and the sea-fog which had come down as a mass of dank mist lifted and then, wonder of wonders, between the piers, leaping from wave to wave as it rushed at headlong speed, swept the strange schooner before the blast, and gained the safety of the harbour. The searchlight followd her, and a shudder ran through all who saw her, for lashed to the helm was a corpse with drooping head, which swung horribly to and fro at each motion of the ship. No other form could be seen on deck at all. The schooner did not pause, but rushed across the harbour and pitched herself on an accumulation of sand and gravel in the south-east corner of the pier jutting under the East Cliff. The very instant the shore was touched, an immense dog sprang up on deck from below and, running forward, jumped from the ship's bow on to the sand. Making straight for the steep cliff below the churchyard, it disappeared in the darkness, which seemed all the blacker since it was beyond the focus of the searchlight.

The coastguard on duty on the eastern side of the harbour was the first to climb on board, and gave me permission with a few others to go with him. We went aft, and our small group saw the dead helmsman while he was still lashed to the wheel. Not often can such a sight have been seen. The man was fastened by his hands, tied one over the other to a spoke of the wheel. Between the inner hand and the wood was a crucifix, the set of beads to which it was attached being around both wrists and wheel, and all kept fast by the binding cords. The poor fellow may have been seated at one time, but the flapping and buffeting of the sails had worked through the rudder to the wheel and dragged him to and fro, so that the cords with which he was tied had cut the flesh to the bone. A doctor who had come on board with us declared after examining the seaman that the man must have been dead for quite two days. In his pocket was a bottle, carefully corked and empty except for a little roll of paper which proved later to be an addition to the ship's log. The coastguard said the man must have tied up his own hands, fastening the knots with his teeth. The dead steersman was soon after reverently removed from the place where he had held his honourable watch and ward and placed in the town mortuary to await an inquest.

Already the sudden storm is passing and is much less fierce; the crowds of onlookers on the cliff are scattering homeward, and the dawn is coming up over the Yorkshire wolds. I shall send, in time for the next issue of *The Daily Graph*, further details of the mystery ship which found her way so miraculously into harbour in the storm.

9 August. Whitby

The sequel to the strange arrival of the mysterious ship in the storm last night is almost more startling than the event itself. It turns out that the schooner is a Russian from Varna, and is called the *Demeter*. She is entirely in ballast of silver sand with only a small amount of cargo – a number of great wooden boxes filled with earth mould. This cargo was consigned to a Whitby solicitor, Mr S. F. Billington, of 7, The Crescent, who this morning went on board and formally took possession of the goods consigned to him.

Later. By the kindness of the Board of Trade inspector, I have been permitted to look over the log book of the *Demeter*, which was in order up to within three days, but contained nothing of special interest except as to facts of missing men. The greatest interest, however, is with regard to the paper in the bottle which was today produced at the inquest, and a more strange narrative than the two between them unfold I have never before come across. I am permitted to use them, and send you a copy herewith. A clerk in the Russian consulate here has very kindly dictated a translation into English for me.

LOG OF THE *DEMETER*. VARNA TO WHITBY.

On 6 July we finished taking in cargo, silver sand and boxes of earth. At noon we set sail. East wind, fresh. Crew, five hands . . . two mates, cook and myself (captain).

On 11 July at dawn entered Bosphorus. Boarded by Turkish Customs officers. All correct. Under way at 4 p.m.

On 12 July through Dardanelles. More Customs officers. At dark passed into Archipelago.

On 13 July passed Cape Matapan. Crew unhappy about something. Seemed scared but would not speak out.

On 14 July was somewhat anxious about crew. Men all steady fellows who sailed with me before. Mate could not make out what was wrong; they only told him there was *something*, and crossed themselves. Mate lost temper with one of them that day and struck him. Expected fierce quarrel, but all was quiet.

On 16 July mate reported in the morning that one of crew, Petrofsky, was missing. Could not account for it. Men more downcast than ever. All said they expected something of the kind, but could not say more than there was *something* aboard. Mate getting very impatient with them; feared some trouble ahead.

On 17 July, yesterday, one of the men, Olgaren, came to my cabin and in an awestruck way confided to me that he thought there was a strange man aboard the ship. He said that during his watch he had been sheltering behind the deck-house as there was a rainstorm, when he saw a tall, thin man who was not like any of the crew come up the companion-way, and go along the deck forward, and disappear. He followed cautiously, but when he got to bows found no one, and the hatchways were all closed. He was in a panic of superstitious fear, and I am afraid the panic may spread. To stop this, I shall today search entire ship carefully from stem to stern.
Later in the day we searched the ship thoroughly. As there were only the big wooden boxes, there were no odd corners where a man could hide. Men much relieved when search was over, and went back to work cheerfully.

22 *July*. Rough weather last three days, and all hands busy with sails – no time to be frightened. Men seem to have forgotten their fear. Praised men for good work in bad weather. Passed Gibralter and out through Straits. All well.

24 *July*. There seems some doom over this ship. Already a hand short, and entering the Bay of Biscay with wild weather ahead, and yet last night another man lost – disappeared. Like the first, he came off his watch and was not seen again. Men all in a panic of fear. Asked if they could have double watch, as they fear to be alone.

28 July. Four days in hell, knocking about in a sort of maelstrom, and the wind a tempest. No sleep for anyone. Men all worn out. Hardly know how to set a watch, since no one fit to go on. Second mate volunteered to steer and watch, and let men snatch a few hours sleep. Less wind, but seas terrific. Feel them less as ship steadier.

29 July. Another tragedy. Had single watch tonight as crew too tired to double up. When morning watch came on deck, could find no one except steersman. Raised outcry, and all came on deck. Thorough search, but no one found. Are now without second mate and crew in a panic. Mate and I agreed to go armed in future and await events.

30 July. Last night. Rejoiced we are nearing England. Weather fine, all sails set. Retired worn out and slept soundly. Awakened by mate telling me that both man on watch and steersman missing. Only mate and I and two hands left to work ship.

1 August. Two days of fog, and not a sail sighted. Had hoped when in the English Channel to be able to signal for help or get into port somewhere. We seem to be drifting to some terrible doom. Mate gone to pieces. Men beyond fear, working on and fearing the worst. They are Russian. The mate is Roumanian.

2 August. Midnight. Woke up from few minutes sleep by hearing a cry, seemingly outside my porthole. Could see nothing in fog. Rushed on deck and ran against mate. Tells me he heard cry and ran, but no sign of man on watch. One more gone. Lord, help us! Think we have passed through straits of Dover and must be now in the North Sea. It is hard to tell in this fog.

3 August. At midnight went to relieve the man at the wheel, but found no one there. I dared not leave it, so shouted for the mate. After a few seconds, he rushed on deck. He looked wild-eyed, and I greatly fear he has lost his reason. He came close to me and whispered hoarsely, "*It* is here. On the watch last night I saw It, like a man, tall and thin, and ghastly pale. It was in the bows looking out. I crept behind It, and thrust my knife into It, but the knife went straight through It, empty as the air." Then he went on, "But It is here and I'll find It. It is in the hold, perhaps in one of those boxes. I'll unscrew them one by one and see. You work the helm." And with a warning look and his finger on his lip, he went below. A choppy wind was springing up and I could not leave the helm. I saw him come out on deck again with a tool-chest and a lantern, and go down the forward hatchway. He is mad, stark, raving mad and it's no use my trying to stop him. I heard him knocking away at something in the hold, and then suddenly there came up the hatchway a sudden, startled scream which made my blood run cold, and up on deck he came as if shot from a gun – a raging madman, with his eyes rolling and his face convulsed with fear. "Save me! Save me!" he cried, and then looked round on the blanket of fog. His horror turned to despair, and in a steady voice he said, "You had better come too, captain, before it is too late. *He* is there. I know the secret now. The sea will save me from Him, and it is all that is left!" Before I could say a word, or move forward to stop him, he sprang on the bulwark and deliberately threw himself into the sea. I suppose I know the secret too, now. It must have been this madman who had got rid of the men one by one, and now he has followed them himself. God help me! How am I to account for all these horrors when I get to port! *When* I get to port! Will that ever be?

4 August. Still fog, which the sunrise cannot pierce. I dared not go below. I dared not leave the helm, so here all night I stayed, and in the dimness of the night, I saw It – Him! The mate was right, God forgive me, to jump overboard, but I am captain and must not leave my ship. I shall defeat this fiend or monster, for I shall tie my hands to the wheel when my strength begins to fail, and with them I shall tie my crucifix and beads which He dare not touch, and then, come good wind or foul, I shall save my soul and my honour as a captain. If we are wrecked, maybe this bottle will be found, and those who find it may know that I have been true to my trust. God help me now!

The verdict at the inquest was an open one, for there was no evidence as to the cause of so many deaths. The captain is considered a hero. He is to be given a public funeral and be buried with honour in the churchyard on the cliff. No trace has been found of the great dog, to the disappointment of the town folk, who would have liked to adopt him. Tomorrow will see the funeral, and so will end this one more "mystery of the sea".

MINA MURRAY'S JOURNAL

8 August. Lucy was very restless all night, and I too could not sleep. The storm was fearful, and, as it boomed loudly among the chimney pots, it made me shudder. When a sharp puff came, it seemed to be like a distant gun. Strangely enough, Lucy did not wake, but she got up twice and dressed herself. Fortunately, each time I awoke in time and managed to undress her without waking her, and got her back to bed. She never resists. It is a strange thing, this sleepwalking.

Early in the morning, we both got up and went down

to the harbour to see if anything had happened in the night. There were very few people about, and though the sun was bright and the air clear and fresh, the big, grim-looking waves seemed dark themselves because the foam that topped them was like snow. They forced themselves in through the narrow mouth of the harbour, like a bullying man going through a crowd. Somehow I felt glad that Jonathan was not on the sea last night, but on land. But oh, is he on land or sea? Where is he and how is he? I am getting fearfully anxious about him. If I only knew what to do. If only I could do something!

The funeral of the poor sea-captain today was most touching. Every boat in the harbour seemed to be there, and the coffin was carried by captains all the way from the pier up to the churchyard. Poor Lucy seemed much upset. I think it will be best for her to go to bed tonight tired out physically, so I shall take her for a long walk by the cliffs to Robin Hood's Bay and back. Perhaps then, she will be less likely to sleepwalk.

Chapter VI

MINA MURRAY'S JOURNAL – CONTINUED

11 August. 3 a.m. I cannot sleep, so I may as well write. I thought that Lucy was better, but tonight we have had such an adventure, such an agonizing experience. Lucy and I were tired, and we fell asleep almost as soon as we climbed into our beds. I do not know how long I slept, but suddenly I became wide awake and sat up with a horrible sense of fear upon me and of some feeling of emptiness around me. The room was dark, so I could not see Lucy's bed; I stole across and felt for her. The bed was empty. I lit a match and found that she was not in the room. The door was shut, but not locked as I had left it. I feared to wake her mother, who has not been at all well lately, so I threw on some clothes and got ready to look for her. As I was leaving the room, it struck me that the clothes she wore might give me some clue to her whereabouts. Dressing-gown would mean house; dress outside. Dressing-gown and dress were both in their places. "Thank God," I said to myself, "she cannot be far, as she is only in her nightdress."

I ran downstairs and looked in the sitting-room. Not there! Then I looked in all the other open rooms of the house, with an ever-growing fear chilling my heart. Finally I came to the hall door and found it open. It was not wide open, but the catch of the lock had not caught. The people of the house are careful to lock the door every night, so I feared that Lucy must have gone out just as she was. I took a big heavy shawl and ran out. The clock was striking one as I was in the Crescent, and there was not a soul in sight. I ran along the North Terrace, but could see no sign of the white figure which I expected. At the edge of the West Cliff above the pier, I looked across the harbour to the East Cliff, in hope or fear – I don't know which – to our favourite seat. We sat there every day. There was a bright full moon and heavy, black driving clouds. For a moment or two I could see nothing, as the shadow of a cloud hid St Mary's Church and all around it. Then, as the cloud passed, I could see the ruins of the abbey coming into view, and the church and churchyard became gradually visible, and there, on our favourite seat, lit up by the silver light of the moon, was a half-reclining figure, snowy white. At that moment a cloud shut out the light, but is seemed to me as though something dark stood behind the seat where the white figure shone, and bent over it. What it was, whether man or beast, I could not tell. I did not wait to catch another glance, but flew down the steep steps to the pier and along by the fish-market to the bridge, which was the only way to reach the East Cliff.

It seemed a long way and that it took an age. I was breathing hard as I toiled up the endless steps to the abbey. When I got almost to the top, I could see the seat and the white figure, and there was undoubtedly something long and black bending over it. I called in fright, "Lucy! Lucy!" and something raised a head, and from where I was I could see a white face and red, gleaming eyes. Lucy did not answer, and I ran on to the entrance of the churchyard. As I entered, the church was between me and the seat, and for a minute or so I lost sight of her. When I came in view again the cloud had passed, and the light of the moon was so brilliant that I could see Lucy half lying down with her head over the back of the seat. She was quite alone, and there was not a sign of any living thing about.

When I bent over her, I could see that she was still asleep. Her red lips parted, and she was breathing – not softly as was usual with her, but in long, heavy gasps, as though striving to get her lungs full at every breath. As I came close, she put up her hand in her sleep and pulled the collar of her nightdress close around her throat. As she did so, she shivered. I flung the warm shawl over her and fastened it at her throat with a big safety pin. I must have been clumsy in my anxiety and pinched or pricked her with it, for, presently, when her breathing became quieter, she put her hand to her throat again and moaned. I began very gently to wake her. She trembled a little and clung to me, and when I told her to come at once with me home, she rose without a word, with the obedience of a child.

Fortune favoured us, and we got home without meeting a soul. We said a prayer of thankfulness, and I tucked Lucy into bed. Before falling asleep, she implored me not to say a word to anyone, even her mother, about her sleep-walking adventure. I promised. I hope I did right. I have locked the door and the key is tied to my wrist, so perhaps I shall not again be disturbed. Lucy is sleeping soundly and the dawn is coming up.

Same day. Noon. All goes well. Lucy slept till I woke her, not even turning over. The adventure of the night does not seem to have harmed her; on the contrary, she looks better this morning than she had done for weeks. I was sorry to notice that my clumsiness with the safety-pin had hurt her. There are two little red points like pin-pricks on the skin of her throat and a drop of blood on the band of her nightdress. When I said how sorry I was, she laughed and cuddled me, and said she did not even feel it. Fortunately it cannot leave a scar as the pricks are so tiny.

Same day. Night. We passed a happy day. The air was clear and the sun bright, and there was a cool breeze. We took our lunch to Mulgrave Woods, Mrs Westenra, who seems a little better, driving by the road, and Lucy and I walking by the cliff path and joining her at the gate. I felt rather sad myself, for I could not help thinking how wonderful it would have been if Jonathan had been with me. I must try to be patient. In the evening we strolled in the Casino Terrace and heard some good music and went to bed early. Lucy seems more restful than she has been for some time, and fell asleep at once. I shall lock the door and keep the key with me as I did before, though I do not expect any trouble tonight.

12 August. I was wrong. Twice during the night I was awakened by Lucy trying to get out. She seemed, even in her sleep, to be a little impatient at finding the door shut, and went back to bed under a sort of protest. I woke with the dawn and heard the birds chirping outside the window. Lucy woke too, and seemed happy. She came and snuggled in beside me and told me about Arthur. I told her how anxious I was about Jonathan, and then she tried to comfort me. Well, she succeeded somewhat, for, though sympathy can't alter facts, it can help to make them more bearable.

13 August. Another quiet day, and to bed with the key on my wrist as before. Again I woke in the night, and found Lucy sitting up in bed, still asleep, pointing to the window. I got up quietly and, pulling aside the blind, looked out. It was brilliant moonlight, and the soft effect of the light over the sea and sky – merged in one great silent mystery – was beautiful beyond words. Between me and the moonlight flitted a great bat, coming and going in great whirling circles. Once or twice it came quite close, but was, I suppose, frightened at seeing me, and flitted away across the harbour towards the abbey. When I came back from the window, Lucy had lain down again and was sleeping peacefully. She did not stir again all night.

14 August. On the East Cliff, reading and writing all day. Lucy seems to love it there as much as I do, and it is hard to get her away from it when it is time to come home for lunch or tea or dinner. This afternoon she made a funny remark. We were coming home for dinner and had come to the top of the steps up from the West Pier and stopped to look at the view as we generally do. The setting sun, low down in the sky, threw a red light over the East Cliff and the old abbey, and seemed to bathe everything in a beautiful, rosy glow. We were silent for a while, and suddenly Lucy murmured, as if to herself, "His red eyes again! They are just the same." I turned a little, so as to look at Lucy without seeming to stare at her, and saw that she was in a half-dreamy state, with an odd look on her face that I could not quite make out. I said nothing, but followed her eyes. She appeared to be looking at our own special seat on which was a dark figure seated alone. I was a little startled myself, for it seemed for an instant as if the stranger had great eyes like burning flames, but then I thought perhaps it was the reflection of the red sun from the windows of St Mary's Church behind our seat. All the same I felt uneasy, and we went back to dinner without speaking. Lucy had a headache and went early to bed. I saw her asleep and went out for a stroll by myself. It was bright moonlight. When I came home, I threw a glance up at our window and saw Lucy's head leaning out. I waved, but she did not notice me or make any movement. As I drew closer, I saw that she was lying with her head up against the window-sill and her eyes shut. She was fast asleep, and by her, seated on the window-sill, was something that looked like a big bird. I ran upstairs, but as I came into the room she was moving back to her bed, fast asleep and breathing heavily. She was holding her hand to her throat, as though to protect it from cold.

I did not wake her, but tucked her up warmly. I have taken care that the door is locked and the window securely fastened.

She looks so sweet as she sleeps, but she is paler than usual and there is a drawn, haggard look under her eyes which I do not like. I fear she is worrying about something. I wish I could find out what it is.

15 August. Rose later than usual. Lucy was languid and tired and slept on after we had been called. We had a happy surprise at breakfast. Arthur's father, who had been ill, was better and wrote to say he would like the marriage to come off soon. Lucy is full of quiet joy, and her mother is glad and sorry at the same time. Later in the day she told me why this was. She is sad to lose Lucy as her very own, but glad she will have a good man to protect her. She is not really better, her heart is getting weaker and her doctor has told her she may die within months. Poor lady. How glad I am that I never told her about Lucy's sleep-walking. A sudden shock might kill her. Lucy is not to know.

17 August. No diary for two whole days. I have not had the heart to write. A shadow seems to be falling over our happiness. No news from Jonathan, and Lucy seems to be growing weaker while her poor mother seems worse day by day. I do not understand Lucy's fading away as she is doing. She eats well and sleeps well, and enjoys the fresh air, but all the time the roses in her cheeks are fading and she gets weaker and more tired every day, and at night I hear her gasping for air. I keep the key of our door always fastened to my wrist at night, but she gets up and walks about the room, and sits at the open window. Last night I found her leaning out when I woke up, and when I tried to wake her, I could not. She was in a faint. When I managed to revive her, she was weak as water, and cried silently between long painful struggles for breath. When I asked her how she came to be at the window she shook her head and turned away. I trust her feeling ill may not be from that unlucky prick of the safety-pin. I looked at her throat just now as she lay asleep, and the tiny wounds did not seem to be healed. They are still open, and, if anything, larger than before, and the edges of them are faintly white. They are like little white dots with red centres. Unless they heal within a day or two, I shall insist that a doctor sees them.

Letter, Samuel F. Billington and Son, Solicitors, Whitby, to Messrs. Carter, Paterson and Co., London.

17 August.

Dear Sirs,

Herewith please receive invoice for goods sent by

Great Northern Railway to King's Cross. These goods are to be delivered to Carfax, near Purfleet, immediately after collection at goods station King's Cross. The house is at present empty, but enclosed please find keys, all of which are labelled.

The goods consist of fifty boxes, and they are to be deposited in the partly ruined building which forms part of the house and was once the ancient chapel of the mansion. The boxes leave by the 10.30 tonight and are due at King's Cross at 4.30 tomorrow afternoon. We enclose cheque for ten pounds, and the exact payment over or under this amount can be adjusted later. On coming away, please leave the keys in the main hall of the house. The owner has a duplicate set.

We should be much obliged if you could deliver these goods to Carfax as soon as possible.

We are, dear Sirs,
Faithfully yours,
Samuel F. Billington and Son.

Letter, Messrs. Carter, Paterson and Co., London, to Messrs. Billington and Son, Whitby

21 August.

Dear Sirs,

We beg to acknowledge £10 received and to return cheque for £1 17s. 9d., being the amount of overpayment, together with our receipt. We have delivered the goods, and the keys have been left in a parcel in the main hall as directed.

We are, dear Sirs,
Yours respectfully
Carter, Paterson and Co.

MINA MURRAY'S JOURNAL

18 August. I am happy today, and write sitting on our seat in the churchyard. Lucy is ever so much better. Last night she slept well all night, and did not disturb me once. She is in good spirits today and full of life and cheerfulness, though she still looks rather pale. She has just reminded me of *that* night, as if I needed any reminding, and how it was on this very seat that I found her asleep. I asked her if she had dreamed at all that night, and she answered, as if trying to remember, "I didn't quite dream, but it all seemed to be real. I wanted to be here. I don't know why, for I was afraid of something – I don't know what. I seemed to be passing through streets and over the bridge, and I heard a lot of dogs howling. The whole town seemed as if it must be full of dogs all howling at once as I went up the steps. Then I had a vague memory of something long and dark with red eyes, and something very sweet and very bitter all around me at once, and then I seemed sinking into deep green water, and there was a singing in my ears as if I were drowning, and then everything seemed passing away from me. My soul seemed to go out from my body and float about the air, and then I came back and found you shaking me. I saw you do it before I felt you." Then she began to laugh. It seemed a little uncanny to me, and I did not quite like it. I thought it better not to keep her mind on the subject, so we talked of other things and Lucy was like her old self again. When we got home, the fresh breeze had braced her up and her pale cheeks were really more rosy. Her mother rejoiced when she saw her, and we all spent a very happy evening together.

19 August. At last news of Jonathan! The dear fellow has been ill, and that is why he did not write. I have just received this letter sent on by Mr Hawkins:

Letter, Sister Agatha, Hospital of St Joseph and St Mary, Budapest, to Miss Wilhelmina Murray.

12 August.

Dear Madam,

I write by the desire of Mr Jonathan Harker, who is himself not strong enough to write, though progressing well, thanks to God and St Joseph and St Mary. He has been under our care for nearly six weeks, suffering from a violent brain fever. He wishes me to send his love and asks also that I write to Mr Peter Hawkins of Exeter to say that he is sorry for the delay and that all his work is completed. He will need some few weeks' rest in our sanatorium in the hills, but will then return. He wishes to say that he has not sufficient money with him, and that he would like to pay for staying here, so that we may continue to help others.

Believe me,

Yours with sympathy and all blessings,

Sister Agatha.

P.S. My patient being asleep, I opened this to let you know something more. He has told me all about you, and that you are shortly to be his wife. All blessings to you both! Our doctor says he has had some fearful shock, and in his delirium his ravings have been dreadful – of wolves and poison and blood, of ghosts, and demons and I know not what else. We would have written long ago if we had known anything of his friends. He came in the train from Klausenburg, and the guard was told by the station-master there that he rushed into the station shouting for a ticket for home. Seeing his state and realizing that he was an Englishman, they gave him a ticket as far as the train went, and then he was brought here. Be assured that he is well cared for. He has won all our hearts. In a few weeks he should be recovered, but be careful of him, and may there be many, many happy years for you both.

19 August. I am to leave in the morning and go over to Jonathan, help nurse him if necessary and bring him home. Mr Hawkins suggests in his very kind letter that we should be married out there. I have cried over the good sister's letter and keep it next to my heart, for it is of Jonathan. My journey is all mapped out, and my luggage ready. I am taking only one change of dress. Lucy will bring my trunk to London and will keep it until Jonathan and I come back as man and wife. I cannot write more for the joy that is in my heart.

Chapter VII

Letter, Mina Harker to Lucy Westenra.

Budapest, 24 August.

My dearest Lucy,

I know you will be anxious to hear all that has happened since we parted at the railway station at Whitby. Well, my dear, I got to Hull all right, and caught the boat to Hamburg, and then the train to here. Jonathan looks weak and ill. He has been through some terrible experience which he does not want to tell me about, and has suffered fear of things beyond mortal knowledge.

I am now sitting by his bedside, where I can see his face while he sleeps. He is waking! . . .

When he woke, he asked me for his coat, as he wanted to get something from the pocket. I asked Sister

Agatha, and she brought all his things. I saw that amongst them was his notebook, and I was going to ask him to let me look at it, for I knew then I might find some clue to his trouble. With his hand on the notebook, he looked at me and said very solemnly, "You know, my dear, we should have no secrets. I have had a great shock, and when I try to think what it is my head spins round and I do not know if it was all real or the dreamings of a madman. The secret is in this book, and I do not want to know it. I want to start my life again with our marriage. Are you willing to share my ignorance? Here is the book. Take it and read it if you will, but do not talk to me about it. I pray that, in the course of duty, I may never have to read again what I have recorded here." He lay back exhausted, and I put the book back under his pillow and kissed him. I have asked Sister Agatha to beg the Superior to let our wedding be this afternoon, and am awaiting her reply . . .

She has just come and told me that the chaplain of the English mission church has been sent for. We are to be married in an hour, or as soon after as Jonathan awakes.

Lucy, we are married. I feel very solemn but very, very happy. Jonathan said he hoped I would always be as happy as he was then, and, saying this, went peacefully to sleep again. I have decided to leave the notebook unread unless it were for his own dear sake or some extreme necessity.

Goodbye, my dear Lucy. I shall post this at once, and perhaps write to you very soon again. I must stop, for Jonathan is waking – I must attend to my husband!

Your ever-loving,

Mina Harker.

Letter, Lucy Westenra to Mina Harker.

Whitby, 30 August.

My dearest Mina,

Oceans of love and millions of kisses, and may you soon be in your own home with your husband. I wish you could be coming home soon enough to be with us here. The strong air would soon restore Jonathan; it has quite restored me. I have an appetite like a cormorant, am full of life and sleep well. You will be glad to know, too, that I have quite given up walking in my sleep. Arthur is here. We are having a wonderful time and I love him more than ever. There he is, calling to me. So no more just at present from your loving,

Lucy.

P.S. Mother sends her love. She seems better, poor dear.

P.P.S. We are to be married on 28 September.

LUCY WESTENRA'S DIARY

Hillingham, 24 August. Home again. I must imitate Mina and keep writing things down. Then we can have long talks when we do meet. I wonder when it will be. I wish she were with me now, for I feel so unhappy. Last night I seemed to be dreaming again, just as I was at Whitby. I feel full of a vague fear and feel so weak and worn out. When Arthur came to lunch, he looked quite grieved when he saw me, and I hadn't the spirit to try and be cheerful.

25 August. Another bad night. I woke as the clock struck twelve and there was a sort of scratching or flapping at the window. I did not mind it and fell asleep again.

More bad dreams. I wish I could remember them. This morning I am horribly weak. My face is ghastly pale, and my throat pains me. I feel short of air. Perhaps there is something wrong with my lungs. I shall try to cheer up when Arthur comes, or he will be miserable to see me like this.

Letter, Arthur Holmwood to Dr Seward.

Albemarle Hotel, 31 August.

My dear Jack,

I want you to do me a favour. Lucy is ill. She does not seem to have any special disease, but she looks awful, and is getting worse every day and seems to have something on her mind. I told her I would ask you to see her, and she finally consented, though she is naturally shy after your last meeting. It will be a painful task for you, old friend, but I know you will do it for her sake. To avoid alarming Lucy's mother, I would be grateful if you could manage to come to lunch at Hillingham tomorrow, two o'clock, and after lunch Lucy will take an opportunity of being alone with you. I shall come in for tea and we can leave together. I am filled with anxiety, and want to consult with you alone as soon as I can after you have seen her. Do not fail!

Arthur.

P.S. My father is very ill, I fear.

Telegram, Arthur Holmwood to Dr Seward.

Cannot see you immediately. Father worse. Please write or send telegram to Father's house at Ring.

Letter, Dr Seward to Arthur Holmwood.

My dear old fellow,

I hasten to let you know at once that I cannot find anything wrong with Miss Westenra's health. At the same time I am by no means satisfied with her appearance; she is sadly different from what she was when I saw her last. I found her in seemingly good spirits, but guessed that she was keeping up appearances for the sake of her mother who, I believe, has not long to live. The three of us made the lunch as cheerful as we could, then Mrs Westenra went to lie down and Lucy was left with me. We went into her boudoir, and as soon as the door was closed, she sank down into a chair with a great sigh and hid her eyes with her hand. I told her that you were anxious about her health and had asked me as a doctor and a friend to help. She looks rather pale, but as there are no symptoms of ill-health apart from that, I have come to the conclusion that it may be something in the mind. This, as you know, is my speciality and I persuaded her to give me her confidence. She told me that she had difficulty in breathing at times, slept deeply and had frightening dreams but could not remember them. She told me that as a child she used to walk in her sleep, and that when she was in Whitby with her mother and her friend Miss Murray, the habit came back. Once she walked out at night and went to the East Cliff, where Miss Murray found her, but she assures me that of late the old habit has not returned. I am doubtful and do not know what to think. I shall see Miss Westenra tomorrow again. She will meet me at a nearby shop so that I do not alarm her mother by calling again too soon.

Letter, Dr Seward to Arthur Holmwood.

My dear Art,

I have seen Lucy again. She was more cheerful than

on the day I first saw her, and certainly looked better. She had lost something of the ghastly look which so upset you, and her breathing was normal. She was sweet as she always is and doing her best to be cheerful. I still can make no diagnosis. She has lost blood but is not anaemic. There must be a cause, but I don't as yet know what it is. I shall continue visiting.

I hope your poor father is better. It must be a terrible thing for you, my dear fellow, to be placed in such a position between two people who are both so dear to you. I know your feelings of duty to your father, and you are right about that but, if need be, I shall send you word to come at once to Lucy, so do not be over-anxious unless you hear from me.

Letter, Dr Seward to Arthur Holmwood.

My dear Art,

My news today is not so good. Lucy this morning had gone back a bit. One good thing however, has come out of this. Mrs Westenra is naturally anxious about Lucy and has placed her in my charge, so I can now come and go as her doctor without alarming her mother unduly. I will write again as soon as I have anything to report.

Yours ever

John Seward.

DR SEWARD'S DIARY

7 September. I saw Lucy yesterday in her room. She was lying on her bed, ghastly pale, and her breathing was painful to see or hear. She turned her head and looked at me, but said nothing. She was not asleep but was simply too weak to make the effort. Her eyes spoke to me, but that was all. Arthur arrived soon after, quite beside himself with anxiety, and I have told him that I am arranging a blood transfusion.

Later. Lucy has had her blood transfusion and something like life came back to her cheeks. She has had a sleeping draught and is sleeping peacefully while I watch beside the bed. Arthur has gone home for a short rest. He is worn out, poor fellow, with travel and anxiety. I shall take the opportunity presently to examine Lucy.

Later. I have noticed for some time that Lucy always wears a narrow black velvet band round her throat. I have moved it a little and discovered a red mark. I looked carefully and saw two small punctures just over the external jugular vein. I thought at first that she had lost blood here, but for her to have lost an amount to cause such a terrible pallor, the whole bed would have been drenched in scarlet. I could make nothing of it. I considered getting a nurse, but finally decided to watch over her myself.

8 September. I sat up all night with Lucy. The sleeping draught worked itself off towards dusk, and she waked naturally. She looked a different being from what she had been before the blood transfusion. She was in good spirits, but seemed worn out. I told Mrs Westenra that I was going to keep vigil by her daughter's bed. She made no objection but wondered if it was necessary, as Lucy was so much better. I was firm, however, and after supper I came and sat by the bedside. Lucy seemed pleased and looked at me gratefully whenever I caught her eye. After a while, she seemed sinking off to sleep but, with an effort, seemed to pull herself together and shook it off. This was repeated several times, with greater effort and with shorter pauses as the time moved on. It was obvious that she did not want to sleep, so I tackled the subject at once.

"You do not want to go to sleep?"

"No, I am afraid."

"Afraid to go to sleep! Why is that? Sleep is usually something we all long for."

"Ah, not if you were like me – if sleep brought horror."

"What on earth do you mean?"

"I don't know; oh, I don't know. And that is what is so terrible. All this weakness comes to me in sleep, until I dread the very thought."

"But, my dear girl, you may sleep tonight. I am here watching you, and I can promise that nothing will happen."

"Ah, I can trust you!" I seized the opportunity, and said, "I promise you that if I see any evidence of bad dreams, I will wake you at once."

"You will? Oh, will you really? How good you are to me. Then I will sleep!" And almost at the word she gave a deep sigh of relief, and sank back asleep.

All night long I watched her. She never stirred, but slept on and on in a deep, health-giving sleep. There was a smile on her face, and it was evident that no bad dreams had come to disturb her peace of mind.

9 September. I was pretty tired and worn out when I got to Hillingham again. For two nights I had hardly had a wink of sleep, and my brain as well as my body was exhausted. Lucy was up and in cheerful spirits. When she shook hands with me she looked sharply in my face and said, "No sitting up tonight for you. You are worn out. I am quite well again, indeed I am, and if there is to be any sitting up, it is I who will sit up with you." I would not argue that point, but went and had my supper. Lucy came with me, and, enlivened by her charming presence, I made an excellent meal, and had a couple of glasses of the more than excellent port. Then Lucy took me upstairs, and showed me a room next to her own where a cosy fire was burning. "Now," she said, "you must stay here. I shall leave this door open and my door too. You can lie on the sofa, for I know I shall never persuade you to go to bed. If I want anything, I shall call out, and you can come to me at once." I had to agree, for I was dog-tired and could not have sat up had I tried. Lucy promised again to call me if she wanted anything, and I lay on the sofa and forgot all about everything.

The next morning, I woke refreshed and went straight to Lucy's room. The blind was down and, as I raised it, the morning sun flooded the room. I went over to the bed, and a deadly fear shot through my heart. There on the bed lay Lucy, apparently in a faint and looking like a corpse. Her heart was beating, and presently she regained consciousness. There was no time to lose. Leaving her with a maid, I rushed out to the hospital, and within a short space of time she had received another life-giving blood transfusion. I decided not to tell Arthur yet, but to see how Lucy went on. I sat by her bed and thought and thought, but my mind kept coming back to those two small punctures in her throat. What had caused them? I could not fight off a terrible suspicion that there was something here that couldn't be explained in purely medical terms; something sinister that disturbed my mind. Lucy slept well into the day, and when she woke she was fairly well and strong, though not nearly so much as the day before. She chatted with me freely and seemed quite unconscious that anything had happened. Later two of the maids came to me and asked if one of them or both might sit up with Miss Lucy that night. I was so tired and overwrought that I accepted, warning them to make sure her window was firmly shut, said farewell to Lucy and her mother, did my rounds at my hospital in Purfleet and went home to bed. I write this down while waiting for sleep. It is coming.

LUCY WESTENRA'S DIARY

17 September. Four days and nights of peace. I am getting so strong again that I hardly know myself. It is as if I had passed through some long nightmare and just awakened to see the beautiful sunshine and feel the fresh air of the morning around me. The bad dreams seem to have gone. The noises which used to frighten me out of my wits – the flapping against the window, the distant voices which seemed so close to me and the harsh sounds that came from I know not where – have all ceased. I go to bed now without any fear of sleep. I do not even try to keep awake, though tree branches or bats or something sometimes flap almost angrily against the window panes. My window is always kept shut, on the orders of Dr Seward, though it does get a little airless in the room.

DR SEWARD'S DIARY

18 September. I drove to Hillingham and with foreboding saw that all the blinds were drawn. I knew that Lucy's mother was an early riser, and feared the worst. Indeed it was true; the poor lady had died of a heart attack in the night. With a heavy heart, I started to compose a telegram to Arthur, who I knew had been unable to leave his dying father, but now he had no choice for, in her weakened state, the shock of her mother's death had proved too much for Lucy and she had died just before I arrived. She was lying on her bed, her mouth open, showing the pale gums. Her teeth in the dim light looked long and sharp and, as I bent over in agony, I saw that the wounds on her throat had completely disappeared.

Her window was open, in spite of her promises, and I can only think that because of the shock she had had, and her craving for air, she had taken a chance and opened it. There is much to explain in this tragedy. Poor, sweet Lucy!

MINA HARKER'S JOURNAL

22 September. I am in the train to Exeter, and Jonathan is sleeping. So much has changed. Here I am married to Jonathan, our dear old friend Mr Hawkins is dead and buried, Jonathan is now a partner in the business, and we have all the money we need. The funeral was held in London today, for Mr Hawkins had many connections there, and the President of the Law Society sent a representative to attend.

Afterwards Jonathan and I went to Hyde Park, sat there for a little while and then walked arm in arm down Piccadilly. As we walked, I saw a beautiful girl in a big cartwheel hat sitting in a carriage outside an Italian restaurant. Suddenly I felt Jonathan clutch my arm so tightly that he hurt me, and he said under his breath, "My God!" I am always anxious about Jonathan after his terrible experiences in Transylvania, so I turned to him quickly, and asked what it was that had upset him.

He was very pale and his eyes seemed bulging out

as, half in terror and half in amazement, he gazed at a tall, thin man, with a beaky nose and black moustache and pointed beard, who was also observing the pretty girl. He was looking at her so hard that he did not see either of us, and so I had a good view of him. His face was not a good face; it was hard, and cruel, and his big white teeth, that looked all the whiter because his lips were so red, were pointed like an animal's. Jonathan kept staring at him until I was afraid he would notice. He looked so fierce and nasty that I feared he might take offence. I asked Jonathan what the matter was, and he answered, evidently thinking that I knew as much about it as he did, "Did you see who it is?"

"No dear," I said, "I don't know him. Who is it?" His answer seemed to shock and thrill me, for he sounded as if he did not know it was me, Mina, to whom he was speaking.

"It is the man himself!"

Jonathan was obviously terrified of something. I do believe that if he had not had me to lean on and support him, he would have collapsed. He kept staring. A man came out of the shop with a small parcel, and gave it to the lady, who then drove off. The dark man kept his eyes fixed on her, and when the carriage moved up Piccadilly, he followed in the same direction and hailed a hansom cab. Jonathan kept looking after him and said, as if to himself, "I believe it is the Count, but he has grown young. My God, if I only knew!"

Jonathan appeared so distressed that I did not ask him any questions but put my arm through his and drew him quietly away. He came easily. We walked a little further and then went and sat for a while in the Green Park. It was a hot day for autumn, and there was a comfortable seat in a shady place. After a few minutes of staring at nothing, Jonathan's eyes closed and he went to sleep with his head on my shoulder. I let him sleep, and in about twenty minutes he awoke and appeared to have forgotten all about the dark stranger. I said nothing about him, but I fear the time is coming when I shall have to look at those papers entrusted to me and discover the facts of my dear one's journey abroad.

Later. A sad homecoming in every way – the house empty of the dear man who was so good to us, but worse still a telegram waiting from Arthur Holmwood telling us that both Lucy and her mother had died. A blessing for the old lady, but poor Arthur, to have lost such sweetness out of his life, and my dear, dear friend Lucy gone, never to return.

Cutting from The Westminster Gazette, *25 September.*

A Hampstead Mystery

During the past two or three days several cases have occurred of young children straying from home or not returning from playing on the Heath. In all these cases the children were too young to give an explanation except to say they had been with a "booful lady". It has always been late in the evening when they have been missed, and on two occasions the children have not been found until early in the following morning. There is an extremely serious side to this mystery, for some of the children, indeed all who have been missed at night, have been slightly torn or wounded in the throat. The wounds are of a type which might be made by a rat or small dog, and are all similiar. The police are keeping a sharp look-out for straying children in and around Hampstead Heath, and for any small, stray dog which may be about.

Chapter VIII

MINA HARKER'S JOURNAL

23 September. Jonathan is better after a bad night. I am so glad he has plenty of work to do, for that keeps his mind off the bad memories, and he is dealing so well with his new responsibilities. He will be away all day today till late and said he could not lunch at home. My household work is done, so I shall take his foreign journal, and lock myself in my room and read it . . .

24 September. I hadn't the heart to write last night. I was so upset by Jonathan's terrible experience in Transylvania. Is it possible that he could have had a fever and imagined it all? And yet he seems quite sure of the man we saw yesterday, and the Count *was* planning to come to London. I shall fetch my typewriter and start transcribing from the shorthand. It may be my duty to show Jonathan's journal to someone else.

JONATHAN HARKER'S JOURNAL

25 September. I thought never to write in this diary again, but the time has come. When I got home last night, Mina had supper ready, and when we had supped, she told me that she had spent the last two days reading and transcribing my journal. Mina is convinced that the man we saw in Green Park was the Count, although he looks younger now. At least this proves that all I wrote was true. Mina proposes to show the journal to our good and clever friend Doctor Seward. I agree with this. We need help badly, but I am not afraid.

DR SEWARD'S DIARY

26 September. I thought that things were getting back to normal. Poor Arthur is bearing up wonderfully well and has his friend Quincey Morris with him, and my patients in the hospital are reasonably calm and well. I am getting used to the loss of Lucy, who gave her heart to another but did not live to enjoy a happy marriage. However, the wound has re-opened, and God only knows what is to be the end of it. Mina Harker has shown me her translation of Jonathan's journal, that he wrote in Transylvania. She says they have seen the dreadful Count in London, and I cannot help linking this with Lucy's strange death. On top of that I came across a copy of the *Westminster Gazette* and noticed a story about children being decoyed away in Hampstead. It did not convey much to me until I saw a description of small punctured wounds in the children's throats, that they had seen a "booful lady", and that others had seen a white figure flitting through the trees.

I thought immediately of Lucy and the bat-like figure

who had haunted her window, and the little wounds in her throat. I thought of Jonathan's description of the undead Count in his coffin, and I thought of Lucy in *her* coffin, the stories of the "booful lady" and the strange white figure. Is it possible? I cannot bear my thoughts and suspicions, but go to the grave of Lucy I must, although the idea fills me with horror . . .

As it happens, I still have the key which unlocks the tomb. For some reason it was not given to Arthur at the time of the funeral, so I took it on his behalf. I shall take with me matches, a candle, a screwdriver, a chisel and a small saw. I do not like to think of what I am going to do. I wish I had someone to go with me, but I would never ask Jonathan, and Arthur, poor fellow, is in the country clearing up his dead father's estate.

Later. I dined alone at Jack Straw's Castle on Hampstead Heath, and at about ten o'clock set out on foot to find the churchyard. It was dark, and the roads were badly lit, and once or twice I had to ask my way, but there were not many people about. At last I found the churchyard wall and, carrying my small bag of tools, I climbed over it. With some difficulty – for it was very dark – I found the Westenra tomb and unlocked the creaky door. Then I lit my candle and looked around. It took me a little while to find Lucy's coffin, for the candle gave but a faint glimmer, but at last I saw it.

I put down my bag, took out my screwdriver and undid the screws which held down the lid. When I removed it, I could see the casing of lead beneath. With a shaking hand, I made a small hole with my chisel and took out the small fret-saw I had brought. I inserted the point of the saw through the hole and sawed down a couple of feet along the side of the lead coffin and then across and down the other side. Taking the edge of the loose flange, I bent it back towards the foot of the coffin and, holding up the candle, looked into the hole. The coffin was empty. I had half expected this, but it was a considerable shock and I wondered if I was dreaming.

Summoning up all my courage, I decided to watch the churchyard for a while, so I bent the leaden casing back again, screwed back the lid of the coffin and hurried thankfully from the tomb, locking the creaky door behind me and putting the key in my pocket.

Once outside, I took up my place behind a yew tree and waited. It was a lonely vigil. Just after I had taken my place, I heard a distant clock strike twelve, and, in time, came one and two. It was cold, my nerves were on edge and I began to wonder if I should have come.

Suddenly, as I turned round, I thought I saw something like a white streak, moving between two dark yew trees at the side of the churchyard farthest from the tomb. I moved quickly, but I had to go round headstones and railed-off tombs, and I stumbled over graves. The sky was overcast, and somewhere far off an early cock crew. A little way off, beyond a line of scattered juniper trees which marked the pathway to the church, a white dim figure flitted in the direction of the tomb. The tomb itself was hidden by trees, and I could not see where the figure disappeared. I heard a rustle of movement coming from the place where I had first seen the white figure and, running over, found on the ground a tiny child. It was sleeping and appeared unhurt. I picked it up and took it quickly out of the churchyard and did not stop until I had got some distance away. Then I went into a clump of trees and struck a match and looked at the child's throat. It was without a scratch or scar of any kind. Was I just in time?

I had now to decide what to do with the child. If I took it to a police station, I should have to give accounts of my movements during the night and explain how I came to find the child. Finally I decided that I would take it to the Heath and, when I heard a policeman coming, would leave it where he could not fail to find it, and then make my way home as quickly as I could. All fell out well. At the edge of Hampstead Heath I heard a policeman's heavy tramp, and, laying the child on the pathway, I waited and watched until he saw it as he flashed his lantern to and fro. I heard his exclamation of astonishment and then went away silently. By good chance I got a cab near the Spaniards Inn and drove to town. I cannot sleep, so I make this entry. I greatly fear that I shall have to return to the tomb.

27 *September*. It was two o'clock before I found a suitable moment to get into the cemetery. A funeral held at noon had just been completed, and the last mourners had drifted away. Waiting from behind a clump of alder trees, I saw the sexton moving about doing various small tasks until finally he locked the gate and went away. I waited a while. It had been outrageous to open a leaden coffin to see if a woman dead nearly a week were really dead. It now seemed the height of folly when I knew from the evidence of my own eyes that the coffin was empty, to open the tomb again, but I climbed into the cemetery, found Lucy's tomb and opened the coffin as before. There lay Lucy, seemingly just as we had seen her lying the night before her funeral. She was, if possible, more radiantly beautiful than ever, and I could not believe that she was dead. The lips were red, even redder than before, and her cheeks had a delicate touch of pink. Shuddering, I put my hand into the coffin and gently pulled back the lips so that I could see Lucy's teeth. One of the canine teeth and that below it were sharp and pointed, and it was the same on the other side. I thought of the small marks on the necks of the little children. But if Lucy was

undead and engaged in wicked work, how was it that she looked so peaceful and innocent? Perhaps she was only evil when she came out of her coffin at night. And then again, what was the part of Count Dracula in all this? From what I had read in Jonathan's journal I felt his presence strongly.

I closed the coffin, locked the tomb, climbed the cemetery wall, went home and lay on the bed to collect my thoughts and decide what to do.

After I had thought deeply, I knew that the whole hideous business was too much for one man and that, in any case, I had no right to investigate further without speaking to Arthur. I dreaded telling him what I had discovered and what I feared. I decided to write to him and ask him to come and see me and bring that dear fellow Quincey Morris with him. Thus the three men who had loved Lucy might be able to help each other and put her poor soul to rest.

28 September. Having decided to seek help, I have been sleeping much better, and last night awaited the arrival of Arthur and Quincey with a feeling of relief, but also one of dread at the prospect of telling them what was happening and the half-formed and ghastly plan of what I thought we had to do.

They arrived at about ten o'clock. Arthur looked better, and it was obvious that having his old friend Quincey with him had helped greatly after the death of not only Lucy but also his own father. I told Arthur that I knew he must have been puzzled by my letter, and that the business was very serious.

"I was certainly puzzled," he replied. "It rather upset me for a bit. There has been so much trouble around my house of late that I could do without any more. I have been curious, too, as to what you mean. Quincey and I talked it over, but the more we talked the more puzzled we got. What could it possibly be?"

I took a deep breath, looked directly at them and said, "I want you to come with me, and to come in secret to the churchyard at Kingstead."

Arthur's face fell as he said in an amazed sort of way, "Where poor Lucy is buried? What for?"

"I am afraid we have to enter the tomb and open the coffin."

"We can't do that," said Arthur. He had become very pale.

"Lucy is not alive," I said gently, "but I think she is undead."

"Undead! Not alive! What do you mean? Is this all a nightmare, or what is it?"

"I think you and Quincey had better come. You must trust me."

"I cannot understand this," said Arthur, near to tears, "but we will come with you."

I much admired him then.

I explained my suspicions of a link between Lucy's death, the attacks on the children and Jonathan's experiences in Transylvania. I did not know then the exact nature of the peril we faced, but I was convinced that some dark and horrible force was at work and my research led me to believe that Dracula – and now Lucy – was a vampire.

We agreed to go to the cemetery that same night. I decided to take with me a small crucifix which one of my patients had given me. If ever we needed the Grace of God it was now.

Chapter IX

DR SEWARD'S DIARY – CONTINUED

It was just a quarter before twelve o'clock when we got into the churchyard over the low wall. The night was dark, with occasional gleams of moonlight between the heavy clouds that scudded across the sky. I unlocked the door of the tomb and we went in. I lit a lantern and pointed to the coffin. Arthur stepped forward hesitatingly.

"Lucy was in this coffin yesterday," I said. I took the screwdriver out of my little bag and again took the lid off the coffin. Arthur looked on, very pale but silent; when the lid was removed he stepped forward. He evidently did not know there was a leaden coffin, and when he saw where I had cut the lead, the blood rushed to his face, but as quickly fell away again, so that he remained of a ghastly whiteness. He was still silent. I forced back the leaden flange and we all fell back. The coffin was empty! For several minutes no one spoke a word. The silence was broken by Quincey Morris. "John, is this your doing?"

"I swear to you by all that I hold sacred that I have not removed her. What happened was this: two nights ago, for a very good reason, I came here. I opened that coffin, which was then sealed up, and found it as now, empty. I then waited and saw something in white come through the trees. The next day I came here in daytime, and she lay there. You will have to take my word for this. It is after sundown now and perhaps after sundown the undead can move. With your permission, Arthur, I am going to try an experiment." Still silent, Arthur nodded in a dazed way.

We went outside and I took some putty from my bag. With this I sealed up the door of the tomb. "Now," I said, "she cannot enter. Let us watch and wait."

In silence we took our places round the tomb, but hidden from the sight of anyone approaching. I pitied the others, especially Arthur. I had grown accustomed to this watching horror, and yet my heart sank within me. There was a long spell of silence and then, far down the avenue of yew trees, we saw a white figure advance – a dim white figure stopped, and at that moment a ray of moonlight fell upon the masses of driving clouds and showed us a dark-haired woman dressed in grave clothes. We could not see the face, for it was bent down over what we saw to be a fair-haired child. There was a pause and then a sharp little cry, such as a child gives in sleep, or a dog as it lies before the fire and dreams. As we looked, the white figure moved forwards again. It was now near enough for us to see clearly, and the moonlight still held. My own heart grew cold as ice, and I could hear the gasp of Arthur, as we recognized the features of Lucy Westenra, but yet how changed! The sweetness had changed to heartless cruelty. I stepped forward and beckoned to the others, and we ranged ourselves in a line before the door of the tomb. I raised my lantern and shone it full on Lucy's face. We could see that her lips were crimson with fresh blood, and that the stream had trickled over her chin and stained the purity of her white robe. We shuddered with horror. My hand was shaking as I held the lantern. Arthur was next to me, and if I had not seized his arm and held him, he would have fallen.

When Lucy – I call the thing that was before us Lucy because it bore her shape – saw us, she drew back with an angry snarl, such as a cat gives when taken unawares; then her eyes ranged over us. Lucy's eyes in form and colour, but now unclean and full of hell-fire instead of pure and gentle as we had known them. At that moment the remains of my love passed into hate and loathing. I could have killed her gladly then and there. She flung the child carelessly to the ground and it lay there moaning. Arthur groaned and hid his face in his hands. Then she advanced towards him with outstretched arms and an evil smile and murmured, "Come to me, Arthur. Leave these others and come to me. My arms are hungry for you. Come, and we can rest together. Come, my husband, come!" Arthur seemed under a spell and, moving his hands from his face, he opened wide his arms. She was leaping for them when I sprang forward and held between them my little golden crucifix. She fell back and, with a suddenly distorted face full of rage, dashed past us as if about to enter the tomb. Suddenly she turned and confronted us as we held the crucifix aloft and, if looks could kill, we saw it at that moment. I signalled to Quincey to unstop the door of the tomb. He did so as quickly as he could, and the woman passed through a crack where scarce a knife blade could have gone. I looked at Arthur. He was on his knees with his head in his hands. Quincey and I sealed up the door again and I put my crucifix away. We all felt a sense of relief, and Arthur rose from his knees.

We picked up the child, who did not seem to have come to harm and I decided as before to leave him where he would be found by a policeman. Then I turned to the others and said, "We will come back tomorrow at a time when she will be in her tomb. There is something we have to do, and you, Arthur, must do it."

29 September – night. This morning I went out and a bought a thick, rounded stake and a heavy coal-hammer, and I sharpened the stake to an acute point so that it became a lethal weapon. I, a doctor, was conspiring to kill. Yet I knew from what Dracula had done to Lucy that if her soul were not laid to rest she would corrupt others as she had tried to ensnare Arthur. There would be more of the undead cursed with immortality and doomed to prey for ever on victims who, when they died, would themselves become undead and continued the wicked work.

We met at midday and got to the churchyard at half-past one. A funeral had just finished, and we strolled about keeping out of sight until the gravediggers had completed their task and the sexton had locked the gate. Then we climbed the wall. I had a long cricket bag with me, and if the others guessed the purpose of the contents, they said nothing.

I unlocked the door of the tomb as before and we went straight to the coffin and opened it. We all looked, Arthur trembling like an aspen, and saw the body lying there in all its death-beauty. But there was no love in my heart, nothing but loathing for the foul Thing which had taken Lucy's shape without her soul. I could see even Arthur's face grow hard as he looked. I gave the lantern to Quincey, undid my bag and took out the hammer and the sharpened stake. We all looked at Arthur and he saw, as we all did, that his must be the hand which would restore Lucy to us as a holy and not an unholy memory. He stepped forward and said bravely, though his hand trembled and his face was pale as snow, "Tell me what I have to do and I will not falter."

I replied, "Take this stake in your left hand, ready to place the point over the heart, and the hammer in your right. I shall say aloud what prayers I can remember, and I trust Quincey will join me. When you hear us begin, strike in God's name."

Arthur took the stake and the hammer with hands that did not tremble. I held the crucifix and prayed quietly, and Quincey joined me. Arthur placed the point over the heart and struck with all his might. The Thing in the coffin writhed, a screech came from the open lips, the heart was pierced and the blood spurted out. Arthur's face was set, but he never faltered as he drove in the mercy-bearing stake. At last the figure lay still. The terrible task was over.

The hammer fell from Arthur's hand, he reeled and would have fallen if we had not caught him. For a few minutes we were so taken up with him that we did not look towards the coffin. When we did, however, a murmur of startled surprise ran from one to another of us. We gazed so eagerly that Arthur rose, for he had been seated on the ground, and came and looked too, and a glad, strange look spread across his face. There in the coffin lay no longer the foul Thing that we had so dreaded and grown to hate, but Lucy as we had seen her in life with her face of innocence and purity. A holy calm seemed to lie like sunshine over her and her soul was finally at rest. Arthur bent and kissed her. Then he held the stake while I sawed off the top part, leaving the point in the body. We soldered up the leaden coffin, screwed up the coffin lid, and, gathering up our belongings, came away. I locked the tomb and gave the key to Arthur. His Lucy was at peace with God. As we shook hands on parting, I think we all knew that we had another terrible enterprise ahead of us.

My next task will be to see Mr and Mrs Harker and enlist their help. Since Jonathan's adventures in Transylvania, he has undertaken some researches into vampires and such-like horrible creatures. He also has in his firm's records all the documents concerning the strange consignment of heavy boxes on the ill-fated ship which ran aground at Whitby and eventually were taken by Carter Paterson to Count Dracula's house Carfax, which is next door to my hospital. That Count Dracula was aboard the ship, I feel certain, and the tragic events concerning Lucy confirms this. I shall call a meeting and we will discuss how best to hunt down the monster Dracula. May God be with us!

Chapter X

MINA HARKER'S JOURNAL

Our good friend Dr Seward has approached Jonathan and me to ask for our help in hunting down Count Dracula. He knows part of the story, but we have other information which could be useful, and of course we are ready to share it. I immediately sent him my Whitby diary, and we are to meet soon. I think he intends to form some kind of committee. We can then share our information and ideas and can prepare a plan. It will be a desperate undertaking, but it must be done.

Later. I know the rest of Lucy's story. May my dear, dear friend now rest in peace! Arthur is truly a brave man. I will do all I can in the hunt for that evil creature who preyed on Lucy and made her like himself.

Later. We met in Dr Seward's study, having had an early dinner. He took the head of the table, motioned to me to sit on his right and asked me to act as secretary.

Jonathan sat next to me. Opposite us sat Arthur and his staunch friend Mr Quincey Morris.

"I have asked Jonathan to speak first," said Dr Seward, "and he has agreed."

Jonathan reached for my hand and spoke as follows:

"As you may know, I am now a busy man, but in such free time as has been available to me, I have been doing some researches, and I am able to tell you something of the kind of enemy with which we have to deal. There are such things as vampires. Some of us unfortunately have evidence that they exist. Such a one is Dracula. He is stronger and more cunning than any man. He has power over the dead and certain animals such as dogs and wolves. He is a devil and he has no heart. He can appear when and where he likes. He can grow and become small. He can vanish. He can also control the elements: the storm, the fog, the thunder."

Jonathan looked round the table. All our eyes were fixed on his.

"I think," said Dr Seward gravely, "that because of his ghastly experiences, we can assume that Jonathan's researches are correct."

Arthur and Quincey and I murmured our agreement.

"Do we undertake this fight," said Dr Seward, "for the sake of our world?"

My husband looked into my eyes. "I answer for Mina and myself," he said.

"Count me in," said Quincey Morris, a man of few words.

"I am with you," said Arthur, "For Lucy's sake if for no other reason."

We all stood up and shook hands. Our solemn pact was made. I felt my heart grow icy cold, but it did not even occur to me to draw back.

We sat down again and there was a short silence

during which Quincey Morris got up quietly and left the room.

The silence was broken by Jonathan. "We have some advantages," he said. "Dracula loses his power at the coming of the day. He can only change his shape at noon or at exact sunrise or sunset, except when he is in his earth-home, his coffin. My own observations confirm my researches."

"Using this information," said Dr Seward, "we must decide what to do. We know that fifty boxes of earth came in the ship to Whitby and were later delivered to Carfax." He was about to say more when he was interrupted in a very startling way. Outside the house came the sound of a pistol shot. The glass of the window was shattered by a bullet which, ricochetting from the top of the frame, struck the far wall of the room. I am afraid I am at heart a coward, for I shrieked out. The men all jumped to their feet, and Arthur ran to the window and raised the sash. As he did so, we heard Quincey's voice outside.

"Sorry! I fear I have alarmed you. I shall come in and tell you about it." A minute later he came in and said, "It was an idiotic thing to do, and I ask your pardon, Mrs Harker, most sincerely. I fear I have frightened you terribly. But the fact is that while we were talking, there came a big bat, which sat on the window-sill. I have got such a horror of them from recent events that I cannot stand them, and I went out to have a shot, as I have been doing in the evenings of late. Arthur laughs at me for it."

"Did you hit it?" asked Dr Seward.

"I don't know; I fancy not, for it flew away into the wood." Without saying any more, Quincey took his seat, and Dr Seward resumed what he was saying.

"It seems to me that, when we are ready, we must either capture or kill this monster in his lair, or in some way sterilize the earth so that he cannot any longer seek safety in it – a kind of purification, to put it another way.

"In the end we may find him in his form of man between the hours of noon and sunset, and so attack him when he is at his most weak. Mina, I am afraid you can have no part in this, but your support will give us all the courage we shall need."

All the men seemed relieved. It was a bitter pill for me to swallow but their minds were made up, so I said nothing except to thank them for their chivalrous care of me.

Quincey Morris resumed the discussion.

"As there is no time to lose, I vote we have a look at his house right now. Time is everything with him, and swift action on our part may save another victim."

They told me to go to bed and sleep – as if a woman can sleep when those she loves are in danger! I shall lie down and pretend to sleep, so that Jonathan will not worry when he returns.

JONATHAN HARKER'S JOURNAL

1 October, 5 a.m. I went with the others to the search with an easy mind. I am so glad that Mina consented to hold back and let us men do the work. Somehow it was a dread to me that she was in this fearful business at all, but now that her work is done, and that it is due to her energy and brains and foresight that the whole story has been put together, she may well feel that her part in it is finished and that from now on she can leave the rest to us.

Dr Seward went to the hospital to check on his patients, and we then went next door to Carfax. He had brought with him a large bunch of assorted keys, one of which he hoped would turn the lock in the big old door. He tried several and presently found one which fitted. After a little turning this way and that, the lock yielded. We pressed on the door, the rusty hinges creaked, and it slowly opened. We had lamps with us, so after we were through we pulled the door gently shut, making sure we would be able to open it again from the inside. We did not want to attract attention from the road. Once inside, we lit our lamps and proceeded on our search.

The whole place was thick with dust, and in the corners of the wall were masses of spider's webs. From my previous visit I had an idea where the chapel was, though I had not been able to gain admission to it, so I led the way and, after a few wrong turnings, we found ourselves opposite a low arched wooden door, ribbed with iron bands. We had picked up a bunch of keys in the hall, and with a little trouble we were able to open the door. There was a foul, earthy smell in the chapel, but we had to continue our search. We found the great earth chests easily. There were only twenty-nine left out of fifty! Once I got a fright, for seeing Arthur suddenly turn and look out of the vaulted door into the dark passage beyond, I looked too, and for an instant my heart stood still. Somewhere, looking out from the shadow, I seemed to see the highlights of the Count's evil face, the ridge of the nose, the red eyes, the red lips, the awful pallor. It was only for a moment, for, as Arthur said, "I thought I saw a face, but it was only the shadows." I turned my lamp in the direction, and stepped into the passage. There was no sign of anyone, and as there were no corners, no doors, no openings of any kind, but only the solid walls of the passage, there could be no hiding place even for *him*. I took it that fear had helped imagination and said nothing.

The morning was quickening in the east when we

emerged from the front. I took the key of the hall door from the bunch, locked the great door and put the key in my pocket.

The house was silent when we got back, and I found my dear Mina fast asleep and rested on the sofa so as not to disturb her. Later today I shall try and find out what happened to those twenty-one missing boxes. If I can, it will make our search for the Count much easier.

Chapter XI

JONATHAN HARKER'S JOURNAL – CONTINUED

Mina and I are now staying at John Seward's house which is part of his hospital. It makes it difficult for my work in Exeter, but it is best all to be together until this business is settled, so on to the next step.

I knew that Carter Paterson, the carriers, had brought down the fifty earth-boxes from Whitby to Carfax in Purfleet, so I thought it possible that they had also taken away the twenty-one missing boxes later on, but where to, and to how many different destinations? I determined to see Carter Paterson first of all.

When I explained that I was the solicitor who had arranged the purchase of Carfax for a client who was, at the time, abroad, they were quite helpful. They had indeed effected the move. Six boxes had gone to 197 Chicksand St, Mile End New Town, six to Jamaica Lane, Bermondsey – both, I knew, were in the east end of London – and nine to 347 Piccadilly in Central London.

That made the total twenty-one. I asked the people in the office if there had been anyone at Carfax during the loading-up, and they mentioned that the foreman had said they had had the help of a very strong old man with a white moustache. The same old man appeared to have gone ahead during their trip to the Piccadilly house, let them in and helped again with the boxes, lifting some of them by himself. I had now gained a useful bit of information, for, if the Count was able to handle the earth-boxes alone, he could redistribute them himself at any time unobserved. Time was, therefore, precious.

It now remains to hunt the fox and destroy his lairs.

When I had imparted my information to the others, we decided to go first to Carfax to make the twenty-nine boxes there unusable. I had with me my little crucifix which the good old woman had given me in Transylvania. Dracula had put holy soil from graves into his boxes and made it unholy. We must sanctify it again and make it impossible for him to use it..

We entered Carfax without trouble and found all things as on the first occasion. In the old chapel the great boxes looked just as we had seen them last. Dr Seward took from his bag a screwdriver, and very soon the top of one of the cases was thrown open. The earth smelt musty and close. I laid the crucifix on top of the earth. Then we all prayed aloud that God would drive out the devil and make the earth holy again. We asked this in the name of Jesus Christ our Saviour. Then Seward withdrew the crucifix and screwed up the lid again. One by one we treated in the same way each of the boxes and left them apparently as we had found them, but now they were holy again and denied to the monster.

We had left Mina at Dr Seward's house for saftey many times, and I was beginning to wonder if she would be happier at home in Exeter, but she was in as much danger as the rest of us, and I dared not send her away from me.

We said goodbye to her again and went to catch the London train. Piccadilly was our next destination. Just before we reached Fenchurch Street, Arthur said to me, "Quincey and I will find a locksmith. You had better not come with us in case there should be any difficulty, for, under the circumstances, it wouldn't seem so bad for us to break into an empty house. But you are a solicitor, and the Law Society might tell you that you should have known better. You had better go with John Seward and stay in the Green Park, somewhere in sight of the house, and when you see the door opened and the locksmith has gone away, you can come across. We shall be on the lookout for you and shall let you in."

Arthur and Quincey hurried off in a cab, and we followed in another. At the corner of Arlington Street, Seward and I got out and strolled into the Green Park. My heart beat as I saw the house, number 347, on which so much of our hope was centred, looming up grim and silent in its deserted condition amongst its more lively and spruce-looking neighbours. We sat down on a bench within good view, and began to smoke cigars, so as to attract as little attention as possible. The minutes seemed to pass with leaden feet as we waited for the coming of the others.

At length we saw a four-wheeler drive up. Out of it in leisurely fashion got Arthur and Quincey, and down from the box descended a man with a bag of tools. I wondered what excuse Arthur and Quincey had given him for wanting to get into the house! Quincey paid the cabman, who touched his hat and drove away. They all ascended the steps, and Arthur pointed out what he wanted done. The workman took off his coat and hung it on the spikes of the railing, saying something to a policeman who just then sauntered along. The policeman nodded, and the man kneeling down placed his bag beside him. He tried various keys and it was not long before, with the help of a little push, we saw him open the door. Then he steadied the door with his knees while the other two went inside, and we saw him take the key out of the lock and give it to Arthur, who had come back outside to pay him. The locksmith touched his hat, took his bag, put on his coat and departed. Not a soul took the slightest notice of the episode. When the man had safely gone, we two crossed the street and knocked at the door. It was immediately opened by Quincey Morris, beside whom stood Arthur, lighting a cigar.

"This place smells vile," said Arthur as we came in. It did indeed smell vile – like the old chapel at Carfax – and with our previous experience, it was plain to us that the Count had been using the place pretty freely. We started to explore the house, all keeping together in case of attack, for we knew we had a strong and cunning enemy to deal with, and as yet we did not know if the Count was in the house or not. In the dining-room which lay at the back of the hall, we found eight boxes of earth. Eight boxes only out of the nine which we sought! Our work was not over, and would never be until we found the missing box. First we opened the shutters of the window which looked out across a narrow stone-flagged yard at the blank face of a stable, pointed to look like the front of a miniature house. There were no windows in it, so we were not afraid of being overlooked. We did not lose any time in examining the boxes. With the tools which we had brought with us, we opened them one by one, and treated them as we had treated those others in the old chapel. It was evident to us that the Count was not at present in the house, and we proceeded to search for his belongings, including, most importantly, his papers. After a quick glance at the rest of the rooms from the basement to the attics, we came to the conclusion that the dining-room contained all we were looking for.

Papers and other possessions lay in a sort of orderly disorder on the great dining-room table. There were title deeds of the Piccadilly house in a great bundle, deeds of the purchase of the houses at Mile End and Bermondsey, notepaper, envelopes and pens and ink. All were covered up in thin wrapping paper to keep them from the dust. There was also a clothes-brush, a brush and comb, and a jug and basin. The basin contained dirty water which was reddened as if with blood. Last of all was a little heap of keys of all sorts and sizes, probably those belonging to the other houses. When we had examined this last find, Arthur and Quincey taking accurate notes of the various addresses of the other houses, took with them the keys in a great bunch, and, taking my little crucifix with them, set out to destroy the boxes in these places. John Seward and I are, with what patience we can, awaiting their return – or the coming of the Count.

Chapter XII

DR SEWARD'S DIARY

The time seemed long while we waited for Arthur and Quincey Morris. If the Count came, it would be better to have four of us there than two. Suddenly we were startled by a knock at the hall door, the double postman's knock of the telegraph boy. I stepped to the door and opened it. The boy handed in a despatch. It was addressed to Jonathan and he read it out as follows: "Look out for D. He has just now, 12.45, come from Carfax hurriedly and may be doing the round, including where you are. Mina."

Jonathan and I were pale but resolute. We prayed that Arthur and Quincey would arrive first.

About half an hour after we had received Mrs Harker's telegram, there came a quiet knock at the hall door. We looked at each other and moved out into the hall. I pulled back the latch and, holding the door half open, stood back, having both hands ready for action.

The gladness of our hearts must have shown upon our faces when, on the step, we saw Arthur and Quincey Morris. They came quickly in and closed the door behind them. Arthur handed Jonathan his little crucifix saying, "It is all right. We found both places; six boxes in each, and we destroyed them all!"

"Destroyed?" I asked.

"Destroyed for him!" We were silent for a minute, and then Jonathan said, "There's nothing to do but to wait here, but if he doesn't turn up by five o'clock, I suggest we go. I don't want to leave Mina too long on her own, and she may have something interesting to report."

"We should have ready some plan of attack," said Quincey, "so that we may throw away no chance. Hush, there is no time now. Have all your arms. Be ready!" Quincey held up a warning hand as he spoke, for we all could hear a key softly inserted in the lock of the hall door.

Quincey took charge, and with a swift glance round the room he at once laid out our plan of attack and, without speaking a word, with a movement of his hand, placed us each in position. Harker and I were just behind the door, so that when it was opened Harker could guard it while I stepped between the incomer and the door. Arthur behind and Quincey in front stood just out of sight, ready to move in front of the window. We waited in a suspense that made the seconds pass along the hall; the Count was evidently prepared for some surprise – at least he feared it.

Suddenly with a single bound he leaped into the room, winning a way past us before any of us could raise a hand to stop him. There was something so panther-like in the movement – something so inhuman – that it seemed to sober us all from the shock of his coming. The first to act was Harker, who, with a quick movement, threw himself before the door leading into the room in the front of the house. As the Count saw us, a horrible sort of snarl passed over his face, showing the eye-teeth long and pointed, but the evil smile as quickly passed into a cold stare of lion-like disdain. His expression changed as, with a single impulse, we all advanced upon him. It was a pity we had not some better organized plan of attack, for even at the moment I wondered what we were to do. I did not myself know whether our lethal weapons would have any effect. Harker evidently meant to find out, for he had ready a great Kukri knife which he had brought in under his coat, and made a fierce and sudden cut at him. The blow was a powerful one; only the diabolical quickness of the Count's leap back saved him. A second less and the blade would have cut into his heart. As it was, the point just cut the cloth of his coat, making a wide gap from which a bundle of bank notes and stream of gold fell out. The expression on the Count's face was so hellish that for a moment I feared for Harker, though I saw him throw the terrible knife aloft again for another stroke. Instinctively I moved forward with a protective impulse, holding my arm, and it was without surprise that I saw the monster cower back as we all moved forward together. It would be impossible to describe the expression of hate and hellish rage which came over the Count's face. With a quick dive he swept under Harker's arm before his blow could fall and, grasping a handful of money from the floor, dashed across the room and threw himself at the window. Amid the crash and glitter of the falling glass, he tumbled on to the flagstone below. We ran over to the window and saw him spring unhurt from the ground. He, rushing up the steps, crossed the yard and pushed open the stable door. There he turned and spoke to us.

"You think to outwit me, you – with your pale faces

all in a row, like sheep in a butcher's. You shall be sorry yet, each one of you! You think you have left me without a place to rest, but I have others. My revenge is just begun! I spread it over centuries and time is on my side. Your girls that you love shall be mine, and through them you and others shall be my creatures to do my bidding, Bah!" With a contemptuous sneer, he passed quickly through the door, and we heard the rusty bolt creak as he fastened it behind him. A door beyond opened and shut. We ran outside but there was no sign of him. It was now late in the afternoon, and sunset was not far off. Our game was up.

With heavy hearts we picked up the fallen money, so that Dracula would not have the use of it should he return, took the title deeds of the house and made our way to my house to thank Mina for her timely warning and tell her that our mission was by no means over. One earth box remained, and the Count alone knew where it was.

MINA HARKER'S JOURNAL

5 October, 5 p.m. Our meeting for report. Present: Arthur Holmwood, Dr John Seward, Quincey Morris, Jonathan Harker, Mina Harker.

Arthur spoke first.

"We have escaped with our lives, but our work is not finished. We still have to find the remaining earth-box and deny the Count his bolt hole."

"We have no clue at all, have we?" said Quincey. "The carrier's men knew nothing of it, and it could be anywhere in this country."

"Yet there is no time to lose," I said. "As we speak, he may be gathering others into his power, and that prospect is too horrible to contemplate." (I was thinking of my sweet Lucy, and I thought that Arthur and the others were doing the same.)

"In this country, in *this* country . . ." said Dr Seward slowly, and suddenly he jumped. "He picked some of the money off the floor. What if he is making for home, for Transylvania, taking with him the last box? We know he has the strength to move it."

"It is possible," said Jonathan, "and I can easily find out. Leave it to me."

I knew that Jonathan, as a solicitor, would know exactly where to go for any kind of information, so we agreed that he should have the next day to make his inquiries, and we would meet again in the early part of the evening.

6 October. Arthur, Quincey and I had a quiet day, Dr Seward went to his patients and Jonathan went off early.

He came back in the evening with a sheaf of papers, and this was his report, given in his own words as I took them down:

"If Dracula wanted to get back to Transylvania, I felt sure that he would go the same way as he came. That is by the Black Sea. I therefore had to find out what ships sailed yesterday to the Black Sea, or were due to sail today. There was nothing in the *Times* list of shipping, but this only has important sailings, so I went to Lloyds where, as you know, ships are insured. Here you will find a list of all ships' sailings no matter how small the boat. I found that only one Black Sea bound ship was going out with the tide, and she was a sailing-ship: the *Czarina Catherine*. She was sailing, or had already sailed, from Doolittle's wharf for Varna and thence on to the other parts up the Danube.

"I found out where Doolittle's wharf was and went straight there, quite prepared to pay for useful information. I found a man in a wooden office so small that the man looked bigger than the office. He was red-faced with a loud voice, but a good fellow who was quite prepared to help me and give me some of his time, for which I duly paid. This man told me that at about 5 p.m. yesterday, a man in a hurry had come to his office. He was tall, thin and pale, with a high nose and very white teeth, and his eyes seemed to be burning. He was all in black and he wanted to know if there was a ship sailing for the Black Sea soon. He was told there was such a ship tied up and ready to go when the tide was right, and he then asked where he could hire a horse and cart and, having received the information, he rushed off and came back quickly driving the cart himself. A big box was in the cart, and he lifted it down on his own, although afterwards it took several men to load it on to the ship. The captain warned him not to delay boarding, for the ship would sail before the turn of the tide. His new passenger asked if there was a ship nearby where he could purchase ship forms, and hurried off. Presumably he boarded in time, though my informant did not see him do so.

"The ship went out on the ebb tide, and by the time I arrived at the wharf, she had sailed down the river and was well out to sea.

"Next I went to see the owner of the ship, who showed me all the invoices and papers. The box we seek is to be landed in Varna, and given to an agent called Ristics who will meet the ship. The owner asked me if there was anything wrong, so that he could telegraph to Varna and make inquiries, but I thanked him and said no, for, friends, what is to be done does not concern police or customs. It must be done by us alone and in our own way."

I asked Jonathan if he thought the Count was on the ship and, if so, if it was necessary to go after him. I dread Jonathan leaving me and going out there again and into such danger. He replied lovingly but firmly that, for the good of mankind, the monster must be hunted down and destroyed, and that it was most probable the Count was on the boat because he had to have the box. I could see the others agreed with him and said no more, but my heart was heavy.

After a general discussion, it was decided to settle nothing that evening, but all should sleep on the facts and try to think out a plan. At breakfast we are to meet again and will decide on our course of action. Shall I go? They might do better without me. I will see in the morning.

DR SEWARD'S DIARY

We all rose early, and I think that sleep did much for each and all of us. When we met at early breakfast there was more general cheerfulness than any of us had ever expected to experience again. In fact it seemed as if the past days had been a dream. Yet we knew we had some terrible decisions to make, and I am going through the facts using Jonathan's own information so that we can make our plan.

Later. At the very outset of our meeting I experienced a great personal relief. Mrs Harker had sent a message by her husband to say that she would not join us at present, as she thought it better that we should be free to discuss our movements without her presence to embarrass us. I felt that Mrs Harker knew that her husband would be going again into danger and did not want to hear about it.

We went at once into our Plan of Campaign, and I spoke first.

"Jonathan is to be congratulated on the speed with which he gathered his information. Bearing in mind the facts he has given us, I have prepared a plan which I would like to put before you.

"The *Czarina Catherine* left the Thames yesterday morning. It will take her at the quickest speed she has ever made at least three weeks to reach Varna, but we can travel overland to the same place in three days. Now, if we allow for two days less for the ship's voyage to be on the safe side, and if we allow a whole day and night for any delays which may occur to us, then we have a margin of nearly two weeks. Thus we ought to leave here on the 17th at the latest. Then we shall at any rate be in Varna a day before the ship arrives, and able to make such preparations as may be necessary. Our best hope will be to come on him when in the box between sunrise and sunset, for then we know he can make no struggle, and we may deal with him as we should. Of course we shall go armed – against evil things, spiritual as well as physical." Here Quincey Morris added, "I understand that the Count comes from wolf country, and it may be that he will get there before us. I propose that we add Winchester rifles to our armament. I have a kind of belief in a Winchester when there is any trouble of that sort around. Do you remember, Art, when we had a wolf-pack after us at Tobolsk? What wouldn't we have given then for a repeater apiece!"

"I think we should go as soon as we are ready," said Arthur. "It will be hard for Jonathan and his wife, but better in the sense that it will cut back the stress of the waiting time."

"I think you are right," said Jonathan, "but either way it will be terrible for her. I will go and talk to her now. She knows I must go and she will not try to stop me." Sadly he rose and left the room. One must admire such love and courage.

"If we are all agreed," I said, "perhaps you, Arthur, and Quincey here might buy our tickets and reserve places. I must go to the hospital." They agreed willingly and, as there was no more to be said, we parted. There is much to do, as we know that we may never come back alive and must act accordingly.

JONATHAN HARKER'S JOURNAL

15 October, Varna. Hotel Odessus. We left Charing Cross on the morning of the 12th, got to Paris the same night, and took the places reserved for us on the Orient Express. We travelled night and day, arriving here at about five o'clock. Arthur went to the Consulate to see if any telegram had arrived for him, while the rest of us came on to this hotel. The journey may have had incidents, but I was too eager to get on to worry about them. Until the *Czarina Catherine* comes into port, there will be no interest for me in anything in the wide world. Thank God Mina is not with us! I know what it means to her to see me go off a second time without her, but after the threats made by Dracula, we cannot risk it. At the same time I cannot let my brave friends go alone. I have the experience and I have an old score to settle with that loathsome monster.

Arthur has just returned. He has four telegrams, one each day since we started, and all to the same effect: that the *Czarina Catherine* had not been reported to Lloyds from anywhere. He had arranged before leaving London that his agent would send him every day a telegram saying if the ship had been reported, so that he might be sure there was a watch being kept at the other end.

We had dinner and went to bed early. Tomorrow we are to see the Vice Consul, and to arrange, if we can, about getting on board the ship as soon as she arrives. Our chance will be to get on the boat between sunrise and sunset. The Count, even if he takes the form of a bat, cannot by himself cross running water, and so cannot leave the ship. As he dare not change to man's form for fear of arousing suspicion, he must remain in the box. If we can come on board after sunrise, he is at our mercy, for we can open the box and make sure of him, as we did of poor Lucy, before he wakes. Officials or seamen here can easily be bribed and should make no trouble. We have only to make sure that the ship cannot come into port between sunset and sunrise without our being warned, and we shall be safe.

17 October. Everything is pretty well fixed now, I think, to welcome the Count on his return to his own country. Arthur told the shippers that he thought that the box sent aboard might contain something stolen from a friend of his, and got a half consent that he might open it at his own risk. The owner gave him a paper telling the captain to give him every assistance in doing what he chose on board the ship, and the same instruction to the agent in Varna. We have seen the agent, who was impressed by Arthur, and we are all satisfied that whatever he can do to aid our wishes will be done. We have already arranged what to do in case we get the box open. If the Count is there, we will cut off his head at once and drive a stake through his heart. According to my reading, if we can manage to do this, the body will soon after fall into dust, thus there would be no evidence against us, in case any suspicion of murder were aroused. But in any case we mean to leave no stone unturned to carry out our intent. We have arranged with certain officials that the instant the *Cza-*

rina Catherine is seen, we are to be informed by special messenger.

24 October. Arthur has just been informed that the *Czarina Catherine* has been reported at the Dardanelles.

DR SEWARD'S DIARY

25 October. We were all wild with excitement when Arthur got his telegram from Lloyds. I know now what men feel like in battle when the call to action is heard.

It is only about twenty-fours hours' sail from the Dardanelles to here, at the rate the *Czarina Catherine* has come from London. She should therefore arrive some time in the morning, but as she cannot possibly get in before then, we are all about to go to bed early. We shall get up at one o'clock, so as to be ready.

26 October. Another day, and still no tidings of the *Czarina Catherine*. She ought to be here by now.

27 October. Still no news. Most strange. I fear the Count may be escaping us.

28 October. Arthur has just received a telegram saying that the *Czarina Catherine* would be entering Galatz at one o'clock.

Galatz, not Varna! I think we all realized when the ship was delayed that nothing would be straight forward; still, it was a surprise. We found that the only train for Galatz went at 6.30 the next morning. Tickets have to be bought and new arrangements made to search the ship at Galatz. It is as if the Count divined our plans and persuaded the Captain to take the ship to a different port, but we are resolved and we will have him yet!

Chapter XIII

DR SEWARD'S DIARY – CONTINUED

29 October. This is written in the train from Varna to Galatz. We are all in an agony of expectation.

30 October. *7 a.m.* We are near Galatz now, and I may not have time to write later. The whistles are sounding. We are on fire with anxiety and eagerness.

JONATHAN HARKER'S JOURNAL

30 October. We were taken on board the *Czarina Catherine*, which lay at anchor out in the river harbour. There we saw the captain, Donelson by name, who told us of his voyage. He said that in all his life he had never had so favourable a run. He said that when they got past the Bosphorus, his crew had begun to grumble, and some of them, the Roumanians, had come and asked him to heave overboard a big box which had been put on board by a queer-looking old man just before they started from London. He had seen them looking at the old fellow, and they had put out two fingers to guard against the evil eye. He thought the superstition of foreigners perfectly ridiculous and he sent them about their business, but when just after this a fog closed in on them, he felt uneasy and couldn't say whether it was about the box or what. The fog went on for five days, and they had just let the wind carry them until, two days ago, the morning sun had come through and they found themselves in the river opposite Galatz. They had lain that night at anchor, but early in the morning, before sunrise, a man came aboard with an order, written to him from England, to receive a box for a certain Count Dracula.

"He had his papers all right," said the Captain, "and I was glad to get rid of the damn thing."

I asked him how the box had been transported, and he told me that a cart was waiting on the quay and that two sturdy fellows had come aboard, one of whom he recognized as a man who sometimes loaded boats which went up the River Sereth. This was valuable news, and I suggested to the others that we should have a short rest to collect our thoughts and then meet for what we all hoped would be our final plan.

Later. I thought I would speak first at our meeting, as I know something of the country and I have maps with me.

I told my fellow hunters that I thought we should follow up the clue concerning the River Sereth. The reason was that, at a place called Fundu, the Sereth is joined by the Bistritza, which runs up round the Borgo Pass. The loop it makes is as close to Dracula's Castle as one can get by water.

"I think we are on the track once more," I said, "and this time we may succeed. Our enemy is now at his most helpless, and if we can come on him by day, on the water, our task will be over. He has a start, but he cannot hurry as he cannot leave his box in case the people on the boat become suspicious. In that case, they would in all likelihood throw the box into the water. The Count knows this."

"Jonathan is right," said Arthur. "I shall get a steam launch and follow him."

"And I, horses to follow on the bank in case he tries to land," said Quincey.

"The Slovaks who run those boats are strong and rough people, but you are well-armed," I said.

Dr Seward said, "I think I had better go with Quincey. We have been accustomed to hunt together, and we two, well-armed, will be a match for whatever may come along."

"And I will go with Arthur on the steam launch," I said, "and pray God we succeed at last!" I felt Mina was with me as I said this and that her prayers were added to mine.

30 October. Night. I am writing this in the light from the furnace door of the steam launch. Arthur is firing up. He is an experienced hand at work, as he has had for years a launch of his own on the Thames, and another on the Norfolk Broads. Regarding our plans, we finally decided, as I have said, that my guess was correct, and that if any waterway was chosen for the Count's escape back to his castle, the Sereth and the Bistritza at its junction would be the one. We have no fear in running at good speed up the river at night, for there is plenty of water, and the banks are wide enough apart to make steaming, even in the dark, easy enough. Quincey and Dr Seward were off on their long ride before we started.

They are to keep up the right bank, far enough off to get on higher lands where they can see a good stretch of river and avoid the following of its curves. They have, for the first stages, two men to ride and lead their spare horses – four in all, so as not to arouse curiosity. When they dismiss the men, which will be shortly, they will themselves look after the horses. It may be necessary for us to join forces; if so, they can mount our whole party.

It is a wild adventure we are on. Here, as we are rushing along through the darkness, with the cold from the river seeming to rise up and strike us, with all the mysterious voices of the night around us, it all comes home. We seem to be drifting into unknown places and unknown ways; into a whole world of dark and dreadful things. Arthur is shutting the furnace door . . .

31 October. Still hurrying along. The day has come, and Arthur is sleeping. I am on watch. The morning is bitterly cold, and though we have heavy fur coats, we are glad of the heat from the furnaces. As yet we have passed only a few open boats, but none of them had on board any box or package of anything like the size of the one we seek. The men were scared every time we turned our electric lamp on them, and fell on their knees and prayed.

1 November, evening. No news today; we have found nothing of the kind we seek. We have now passed into the River Bistritza, and if we are wrong in our guess our chance is gone. We have overhauled every boat, big and little. Early this morning, one crew took us for a government boat, and treated us accordingly. We saw in this a way of smoothing matters, so at Fundu, where the Bistritza runs into the Sereth, we bought a Roumanian flag, which we now fly conspicuously. With every boat which we have overhauled since then, this trick has succeeded; we have had every respect shown to us and not once any objection to whatever we chose to ask or do. Some of the Slovaks tell us that a big boat passed them, going at more than usual speed as she had a double crew on board. This was before they came to Fundu, so they could not tell us whether the boat turned into the Bistritza or continued on up the Sereth. At Fundu we could not hear of any such boat, so she must have passed there in the night.

Arthur insists on keeping the first watch. God bless him for his goodness.

2 November, morning. Broad daylight now. I wish we could go faster, but we cannot; the engines are throbbing and doing their utmost. I wonder how John Seward and Quincey Morris are getting on. There seem to be endless streams running down the mountains into this river, but as none of them are very large at this time of year, the horsemen may not have been held up. I hope that before we get to Strasba we shall see them, for if by that time we have not overtaken the Count, it may be necessary to consult together what to do next.

DR SEWARD'S DIARY

2 November. Three days on the road. No news and no time to write if there had been, for every moment is precious. We have had only rest needful for the horses, but we are both bearing it wonderfully. We must push on; we shall never feel happy until we get the launch in sight again.

3 November. We heard at Fundu that the launch had gone up the Bistritza. I wish it wasn't so cold. There are signs of snow coming, and if it falls heavily, it will stop us. If that happens, we must get a sledge and go on, Russian fashion.

JONATHAN HARKER'S JOURNAL

4 November. The engine of our launch is failing, and we have had to abandon it and take to horses. But for this we should have overtaken the boat long ago. We are following on the track and we have our arms. If only Jack and Quincey were with us. We must only hope. If I write no more, goodbye Mina. God bless and keep you.

DR SEWARD'S DIARY

6 November. No sign of the launch. I hope they have not had an accident. If they have, I think they will come on with horses. We are beginning to hear the distant howling of wolves. It is snowing.

Later. Straight in front of us and not far off – in fact so near that I wondered we had not noticed before – came a group of mounted men hurrying along. In the midst of them was a cart, a long wagon which swept from side to side, like a dog's tail wagging, with the holes and bumps in the surface of the road. Outlined against the snow as they were, I could see they were peasants or gypsies of some kind.

On the cart was a great square chest. My heart leaped as I saw it, for I felt that the end was coming. Evening was drawing close and I well knew that at sunset the Thing, which was still then imprisoned there, would be free again and could take one of many forms to get away from us.

"Look," said Quincey, "they are coming quickly. They are galloping as hard as they can. They are racing for the sunset. We may be too late." A blinding rush of snow came down, but we pressed on. When it lifted, I saw on the north side of the wagon party, two men riding at breakneck speed, and I knew it was Jonathan and Arthur. They too were pursuing the wagon. As we rode, the howling of wolves came closer and closer, the snow was falling in heavy flakes close over us and beyond, the sun was shining more and more brightly as it sank down towards the far mountain tops. In the distance I could see here and there dots moving singly and in twos and threes and larger numbers – the wolves were gathering for their prey.

We drew closer and closer to the others and to the wagon, which was going on at redoubled speed. We could see that Jonathan and Quincey were going to reach it seconds ahead of us. Suddenly a voice shouted, "Halt!" It was Jonathan's and it was echoed by Quincey's even louder order: "Halt! Halt!" The gypsies could not have known the language, but there was no mistaking the tone of the words. Instinctively they reined in, and at that instant Jonathan and Quincey dashed up on one side and, seconds later, we dashed up on the other. The leader of the gypsies, a splendid-looking fellow, waved them back, and in a fierce voice gave to his companions some word to proceed. They lashed the horses, which sprang forward, but we all four raised our Winchester rifles, and spreading out, commanded them to stop. Seeing they were surrounded, the leader turned to his men and gave a word, at which every man of the gypsy party drew what weapon he carried, and held himself in readiness to attack.

The leader, with a quick movement of his rein, threw

his horse out in front, and pointing first to the sun – now close down on the hill tops – and then to the castle, said something which we did not undertand. For answer, the four of us threw ourselves from our horses and dashed towards the cart. Immediately the leader of the gypsies gave a command, and his men instantly formed round the cart in a sort of undisciplined way, each one shouldering and pushing the other in his eagerness to carry out the order.

While Arthur and I covered the gypsies with our rifles, Jonathan and Quincey were forcing a way to the cart. In an instant, Jonathan was up and, with a strength which seemed incredible, raised the great box, and flung it over the wheel to the ground. At the same time, on the other side, Quincey was fighting desperately to get through the line of gypsies. Their knives flashed, and they cut at him. He had parried with his great bowie knife, and it appeared as if he had come through in safety, but as he sprang beside Jonathan who had by now jumped from the cart, I could see that with his left hand he was clutching at his side, and that the blood was spurting through his fingers. In spite of this, he did not stop, for as Jonathan, with desperate energy, attacked one end of the box, trying to prise off the lid with his great kukri knife, he attacked the other end frantically with his bowie. Under the efforts of both men the lid began to yield, the nails drew with a quick screeching sound, and the top of the box was thrown back. Arthur and I were still covering the gypsies with our rifles; they had given in and made no further resistance. The sun was almost down on the mountain tops, and the shadows of the whole group fell long upon the snow. I saw the Count lying within the box upon the earth, some of which had scattered over him during his fall from the cart. He was deathly pale, just like a waxen image, and the red eyes glared with a horrible vindictive look.

As we looked down on him, his eyes saw the sinking sun, and the look of hate in them turned to triumph.

But, in the instant, came the sweep and flash of Jonathan's great knife. It sheared through the monster's throat, while at the same moment Quincey's bowie knife plunged into the heart.

It was like a miracle, but before our eyes, and almost in the drawing of a breath, the whole body crumbled into dust and passed from our sight.

On the face, as it dissolved and vanished from our sight, was a look of peace, such as none of us could have imagined might have rested there.

The Castle of Dracula now stood out against the red sky, and every stone of its broken battlements was visible against the light of the setting sun.

The gypsies, taking us as in some way the cause of the extraordinary disappearance of the dead man, turned, without a word, and rode away as if for their lives. Those who were unmounted jumped upon the wagon and shouted to the horsemen not to desert them. The wolves, which had withdrawn to a safe distance, followed in their wake, leaving us alone.

Quincey, who had sunk to the ground, leaned on his elbow, holding his hand pressed to his side; the blood still gushed through his fingers. I ran to him, but even a doctor could not stem that flow of blood. Jonathan cradled his head as I knelt at his side with my hand pressed into his wound and talked quietly to him.

We were all on our knees by then, as he smiled on us and fought for breath. Then the dying man spoke:

"Now God be praised that all has not been in vain! The curse of Dracula has passed away!"

And, to our bitter grief, with a smile and in silence, he died a gallant gentleman.

NOTE

Seven years ago we all went through the flames; and the happiness of some of us since then is, we think, well worth the pain we endured. It is an added joy to Mina and to me that our boy's birthday is the same day as that on which Quincey Morris died. His mother holds, I know, the secret belief that some of our brave friend's spirit has passed into him. His bundle of names links all our little band of men together; but we call him Quincey.

In the summer of this year we made a journey to Transylvania, and went over the old ground which was, and is, to us so full of vivid and terrible memories. It was almost impossible to believe that the things which we had seen with our own eyes and heard with our own ears were living truths. The castle stood as before, reared high above a waste of desolation. Castle Dracula.

JONATHAN HARKER